HAVE YOU READ THESE NARWHAL AND JELLY BOOKS?

NARWHAL: UNICORN OF THE SEA!

SUPER NARWHAL AND JELLY JOLT

PEANUT BUTTER AND JELLY

NARWHAL'S OTTER FRIEND

HAPPY NARWHALIDAYS

NARWHAL'S

MONODON MONOCEROS

SCHOOL OF AWESOMENESS

BEN CLANTON

tundra

IN MEMORY OF THE KIND, CURIOUS AND CREATIVE CROSLEY JAYNE BUCHNER

AND WITH MY THANKS TO PROF. AMADOU FOFANA, SUE BROWN, GLENDA SKEIM, PROF. JEANNE CLARK, PROF. JOYCE MILLEN, PROF. REBECCA DOBKINS, MIKE MCGARVEY, ALLEN SLATER, CINDY GALVIN AND ALL THE EDUCATORS WHO HAVE CHALLENGED AND INSPIRED ME. ALSO TO TEACHERS WHO HAVE HELPED MY BOOKS FIND READERS, ESPECIALLY MICHELE O'HARE!

Text and illustrations copyright © 2021 by Ben Clanton

Tundra Books, an imprint of Penguin Random House Canada Young Readers, a division of Penguin Random House of Canada Limited

Library and Archives Canada Cataloguing in Publication

Title: Narwhal's school of awesomeness / Ben Clanton.
Names: Clanton, Ben, 1988- author, illustrator.
Series: Clanton, Ben, 1988- Narwhal and Jelly book ; 6.
Description: Series statement: Narwhal and Jelly book
Identifiers: Canadiana (print) 20210090421 | Canadiana (ebook) 20210090553 |
ISBN 9780735262546 (hardcover) | ISBN 9780735262560 (EPUB)
Subjects: LCGFT: Graphic novels.
Classification: LCC PZ7.7.C53 Nar 2021 | DDC j741.5/973—dc23

Published simultaneously in the United States of America by Tundra Books of Northern New York, an imprint of Penguin Random House Canada Young Readers, a division of Penguin Random House of Canada Limited

Library of Congress Control Number: 2020952297

Edited by Tara Walker and Peter Phillips
Designed by Ben Clanton | Coloring by Jaime Temairik and Ben Clanton
The artwork in this book was rendered in colored pencil, watercolor and ink, and colored digitally.
The text was set in a typeface based on hand-lettering by Ben Clanton.

Photos: (chalkboard) © STUDIO DREAM/Shutterstock; (strawberry) © Valentina Razumova/Shutterstock; (waffle) © Tiger Images/Shutterstock; (pineapple) © daysupa/Shutterstock; (fries) © Drozhzhina Elena/Shutterstock; (scales) © Natalia Kudryavtseva/Shutterstock; (scales 2) © HPL17/Shutterstock

Printed in Canada

www.penguinrandomhouse.ca

1   2   3   4   5   25   24   23   22   21

Penguin
Random House
TUNDRA BOOKS

CONTENTS

GO
FISH!

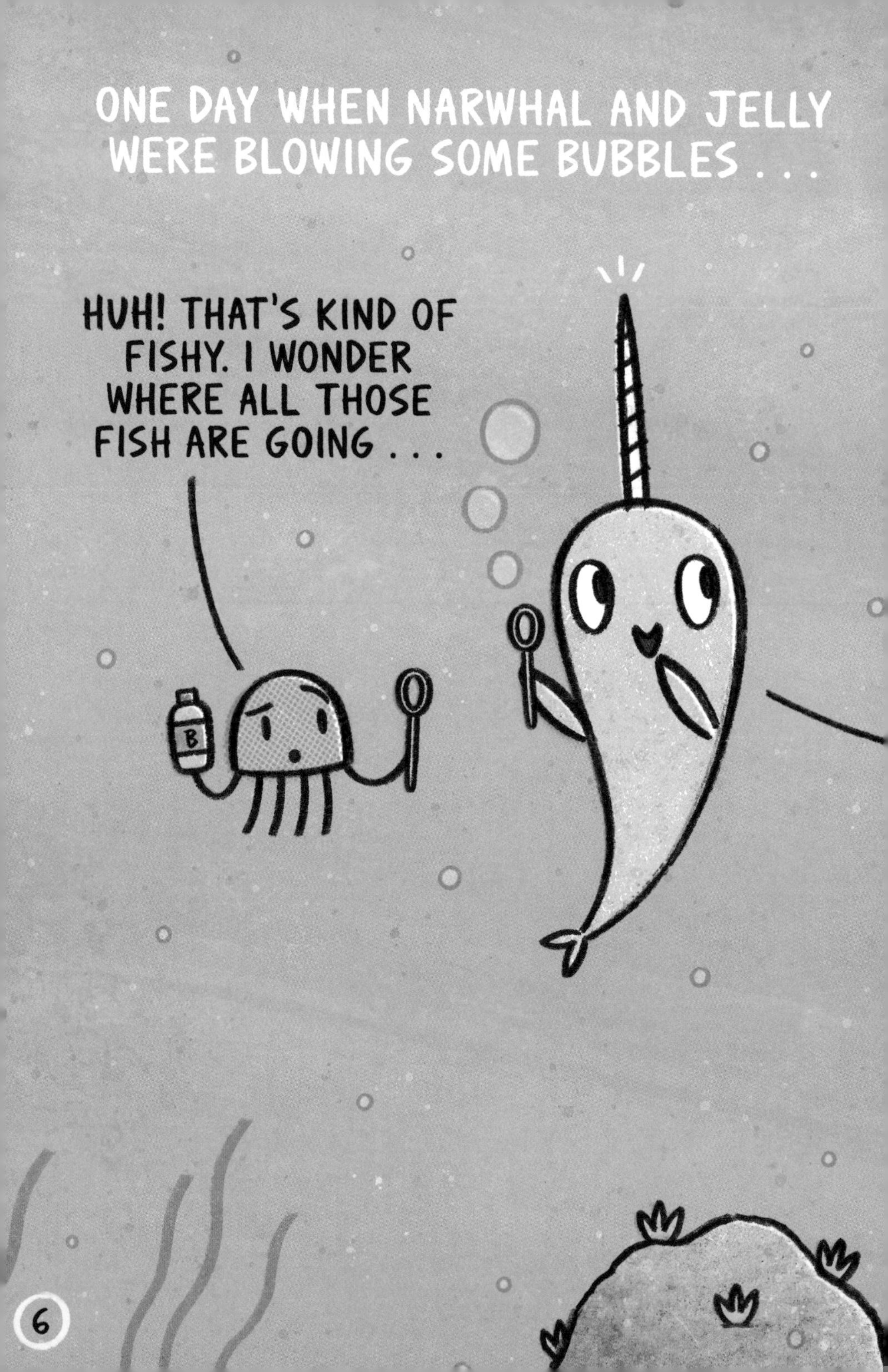
ONE DAY WHEN NARWHAL AND JELLY WERE BLOWING SOME BUBBLES . . .
HUH! THAT'S KIND OF FISHY. I WONDER WHERE ALL THOSE FISH ARE GOING . . .
B

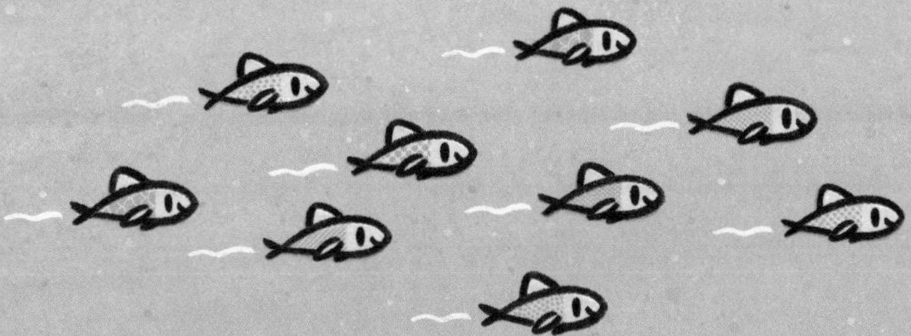

HMMM!
MAYBE THEY'RE . . .

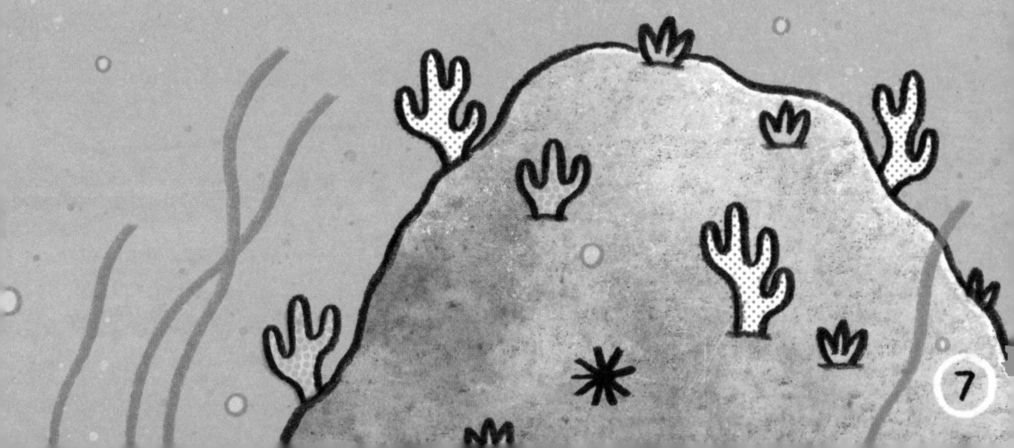

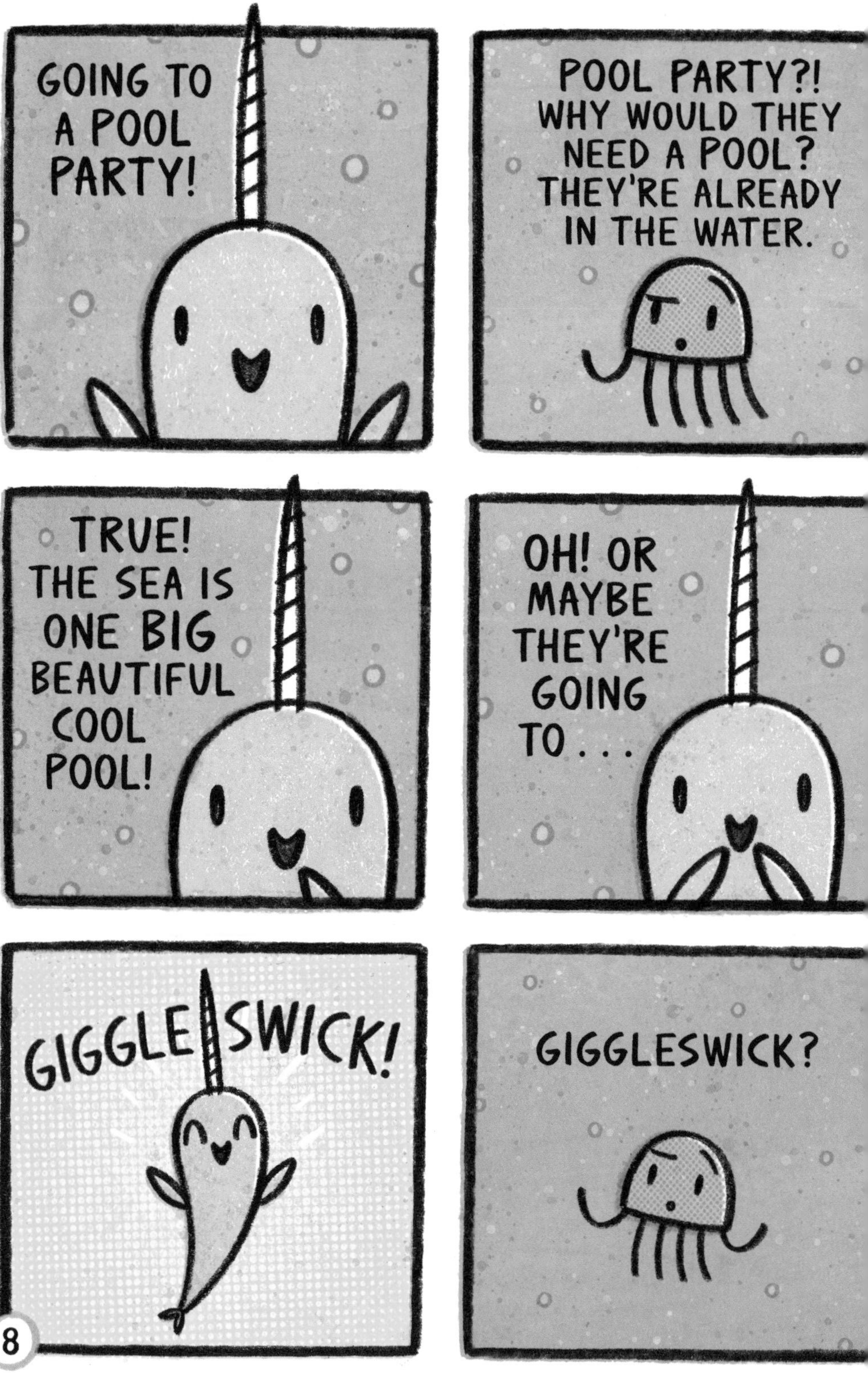
GOING TO A POOL PARTY!
POOL PARTY?! WHY WOULD THEY NEED A POOL? THEY'RE ALREADY IN THE WATER.
TRUE! THE SEA IS ONE BIG BEAUTIFUL COOL POOL!
OH! OR MAYBE THEY'RE GOING TO . . .
GIGGLESWICK!
GIGGLESWICK?

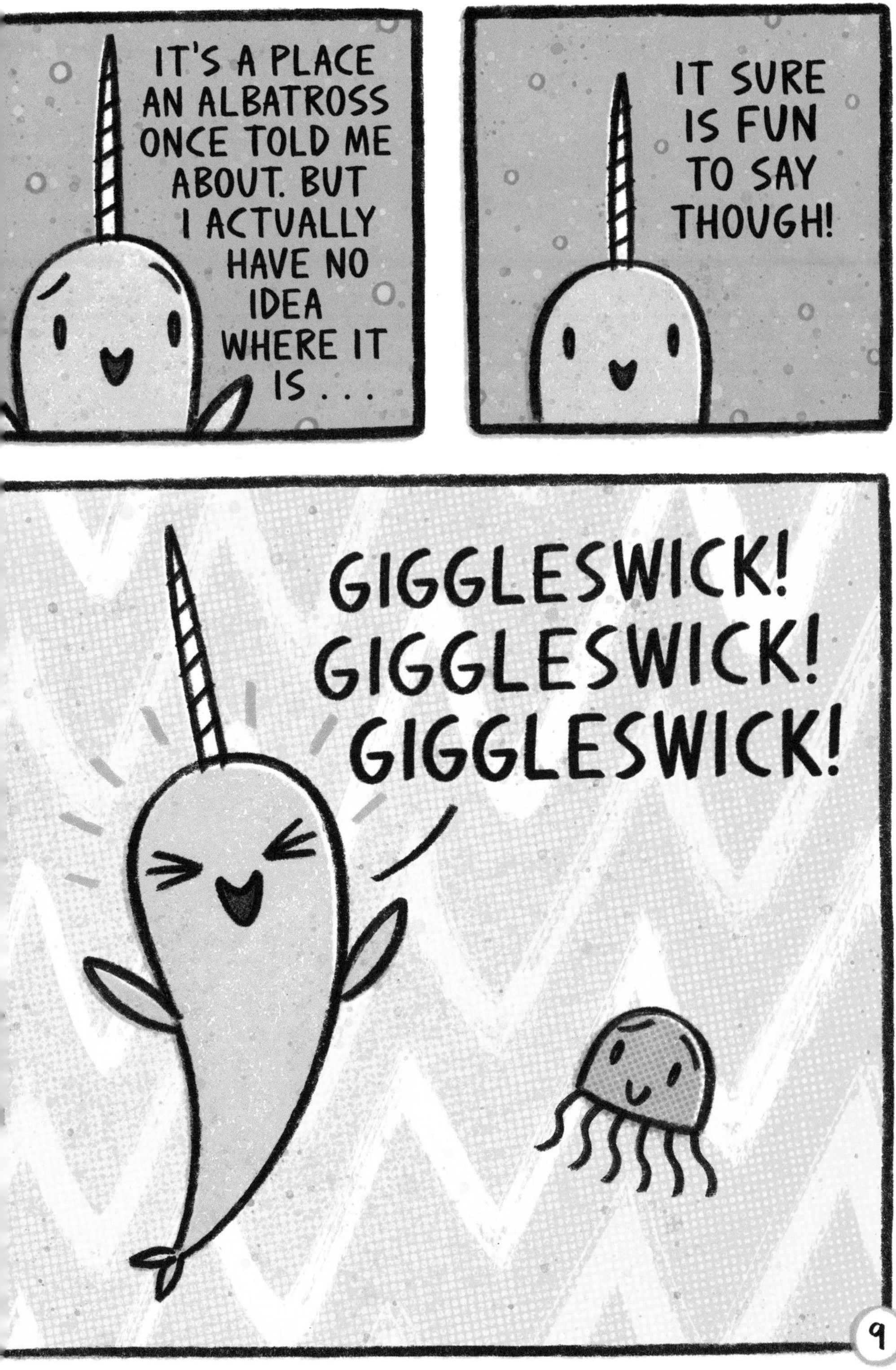
IT'S A PLACE AN ALBATROSS ONCE TOLD ME ABOUT. BUT I ACTUALLY HAVE NO IDEA WHERE IT IS . . .
IT SURE IS FUN TO SAY THOUGH!
GIGGLESWICK! GIGGLESWICK! GIGGLESWICK!

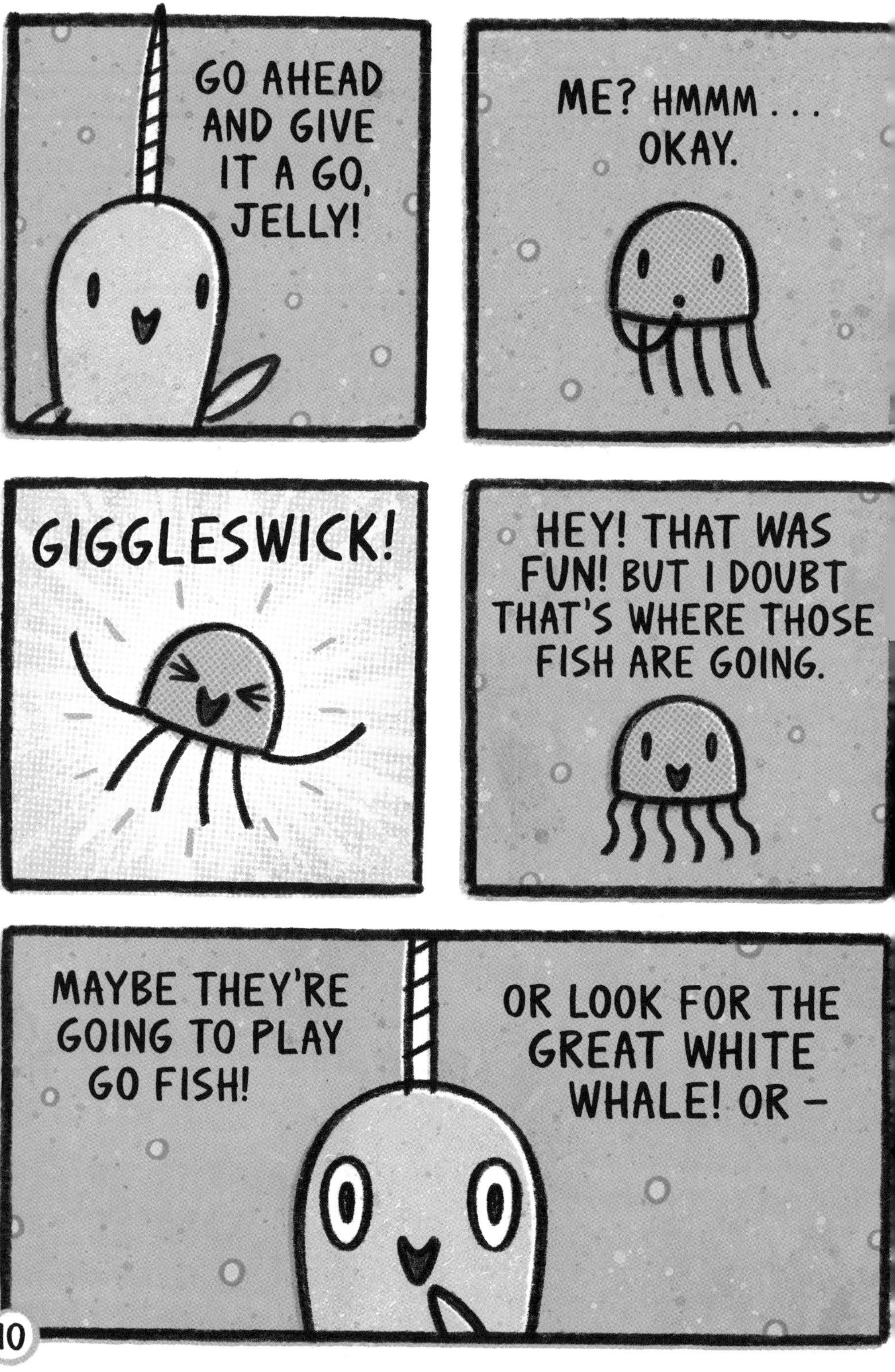
GO AHEAD AND GIVE IT A GO, JELLY!
ME? HMMM . . . OKAY.
GIGGLESWICK!
HEY! THAT WAS FUN! BUT I DOUBT THAT'S WHERE THOSE FISH ARE GOING.
MAYBE THEY'RE GOING TO PLAY GO FISH!
OR LOOK FOR THE GREAT WHITE WHALE! OR –

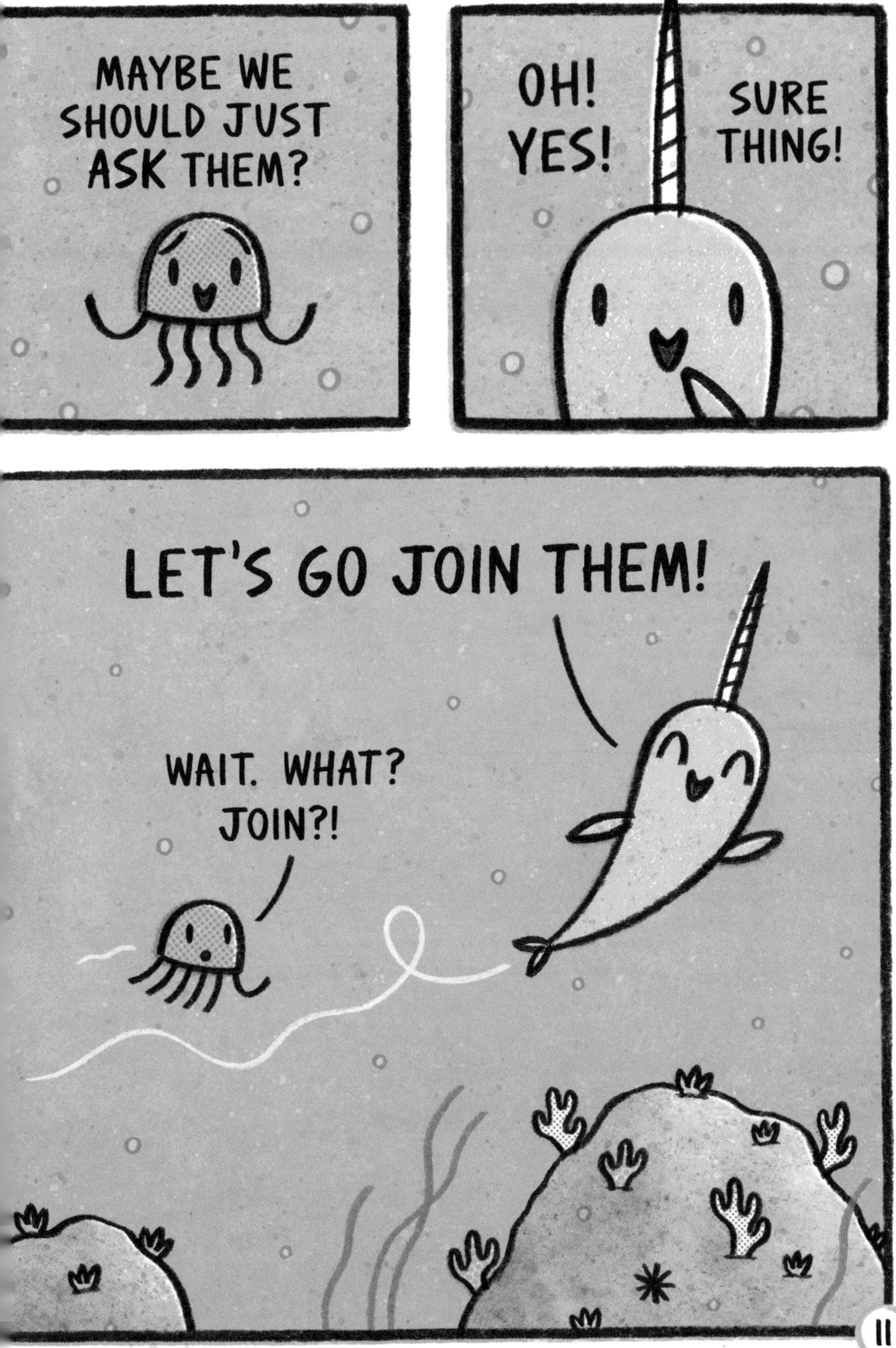
MAYBE WE SHOULD JUST ASK THEM?
OH! YES!
SURE THING!
LET'S GO JOIN THEM!
WAIT. WHAT? JOIN?!

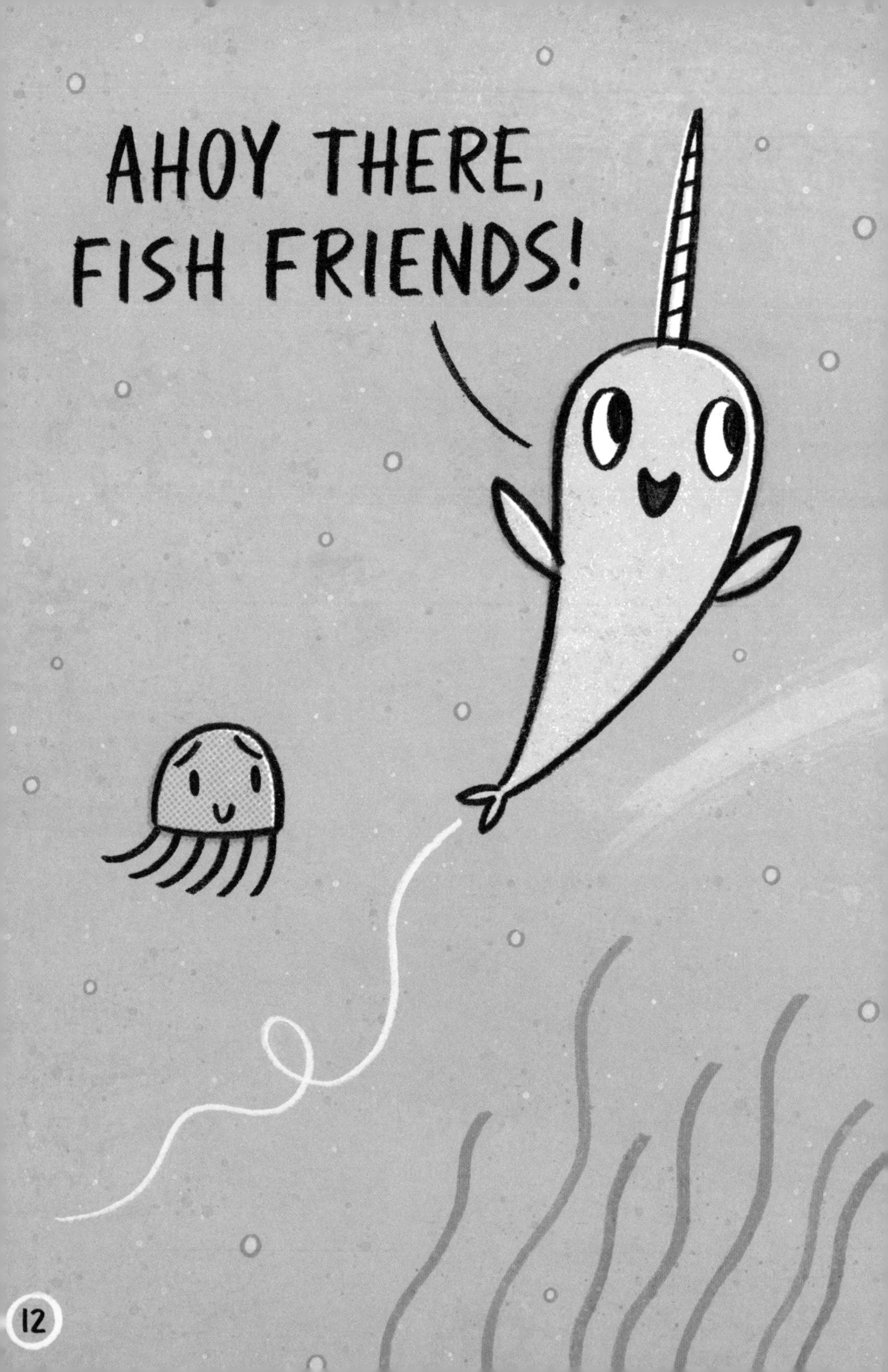
AHOY THERE, FISH FRIENDS!

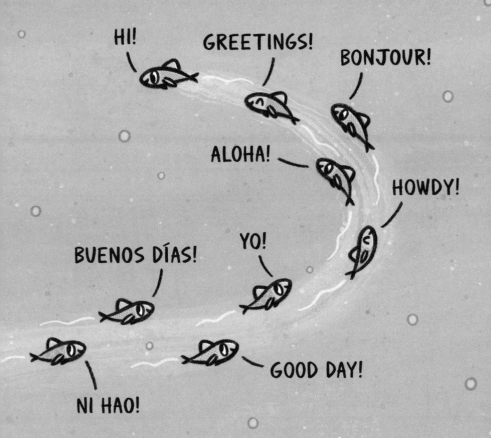

HI!

GREETINGS!

BONJOUR!

ALOHA!

HOWDY!

BUENOS DÍAS!

YO!

NI HAO!

GOOD DAY!

I'M NARWHAL THE NARWHAL!

UNICORN OF THE SEA!

UM . . . HI. I'M JELLY.

THE JELLYFISH.

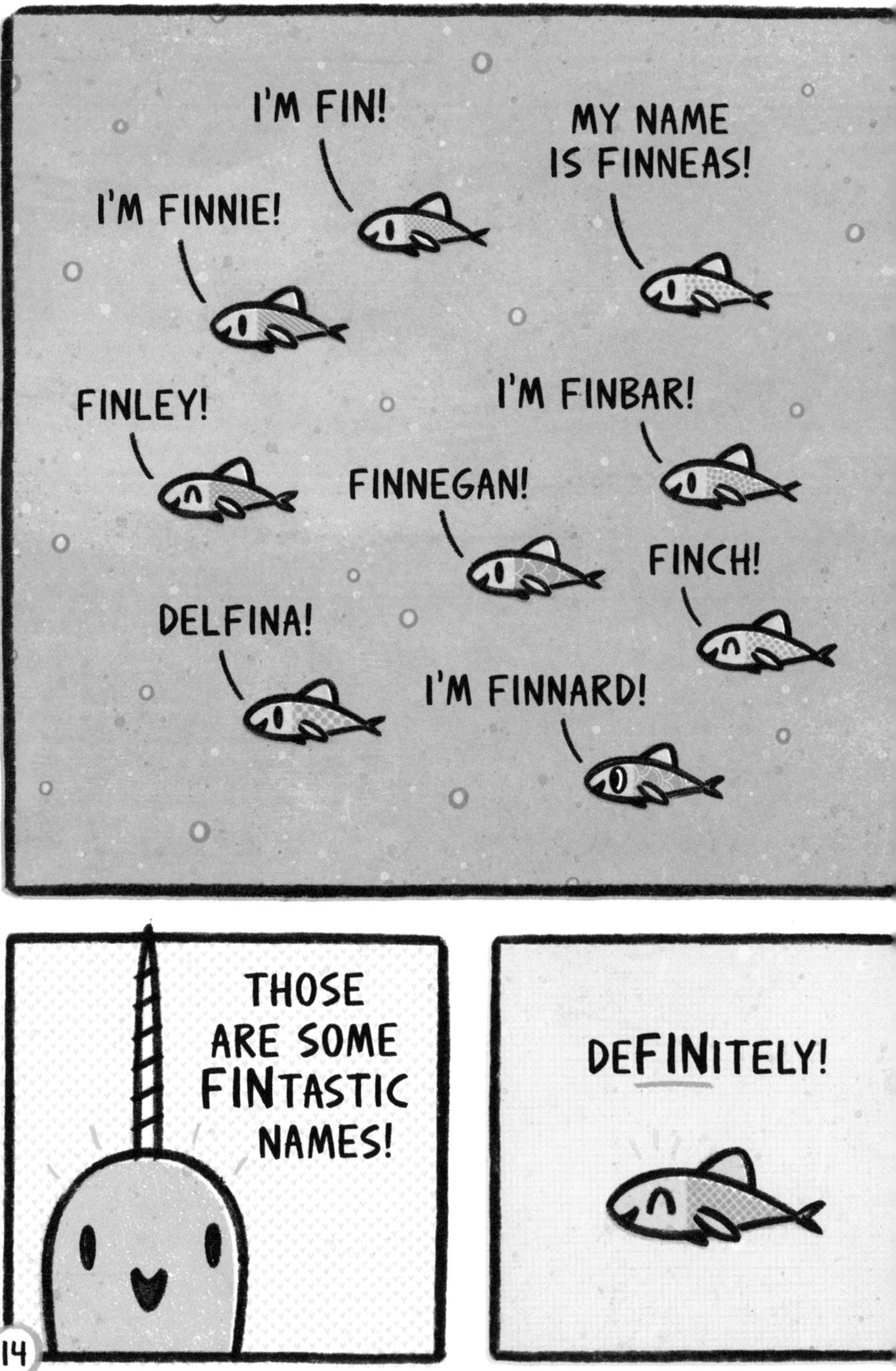
I'M FIN!
MY NAME IS FINNEAS!
I'M FINNIE!
FINLEY!
I'M FINBAR!
FINNEGAN!
FINCH!
DELFINA!
I'M FINNARD!
THOSE ARE SOME FINTASTIC NAMES!
DEFINITELY!

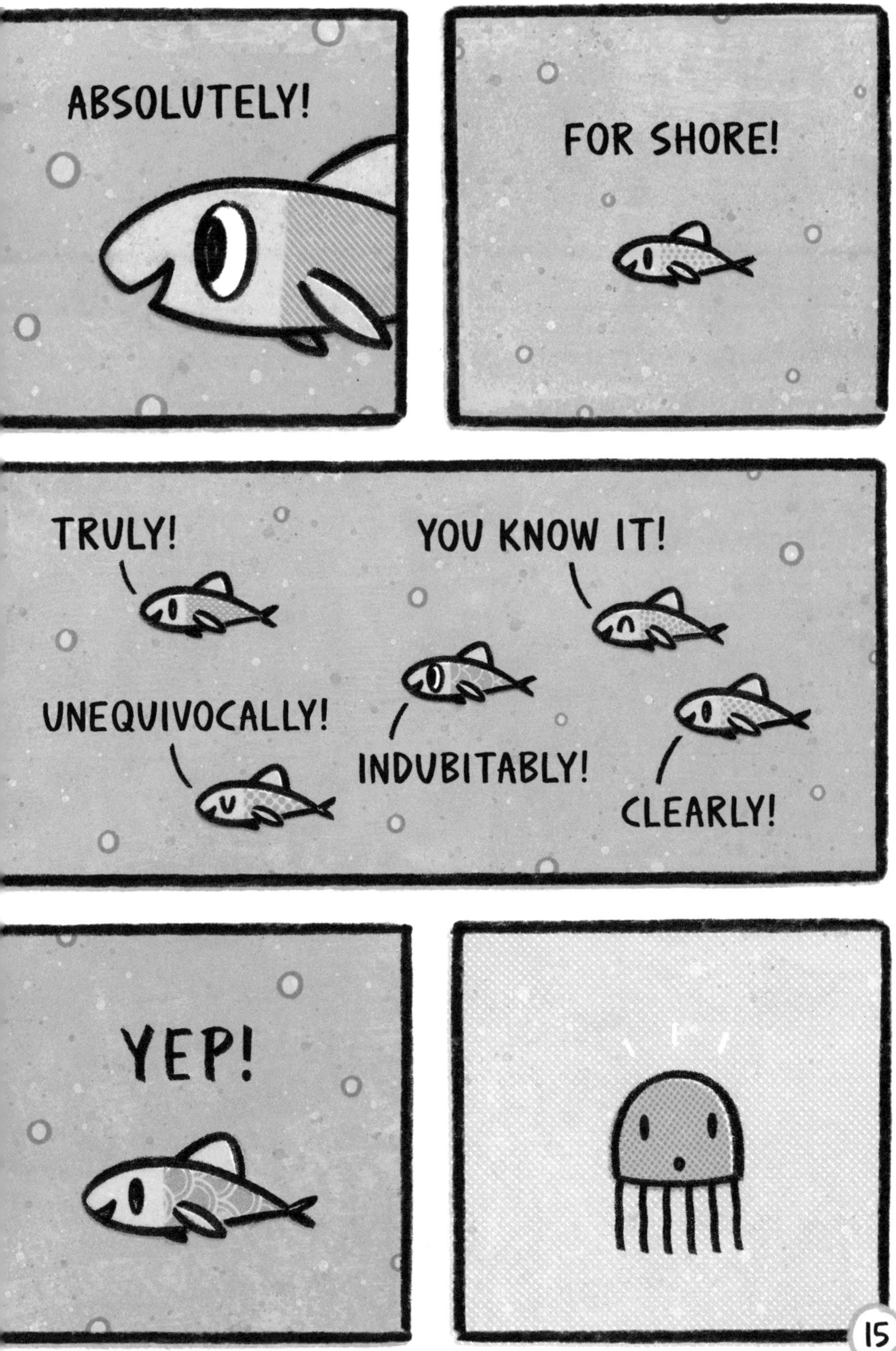
ABSOLUTELY!
FOR SHORE!
TRULY!
YOU KNOW IT!
UNEQUIVOCALLY!
INDUBITABLY!
CLEARLY!
YEP!

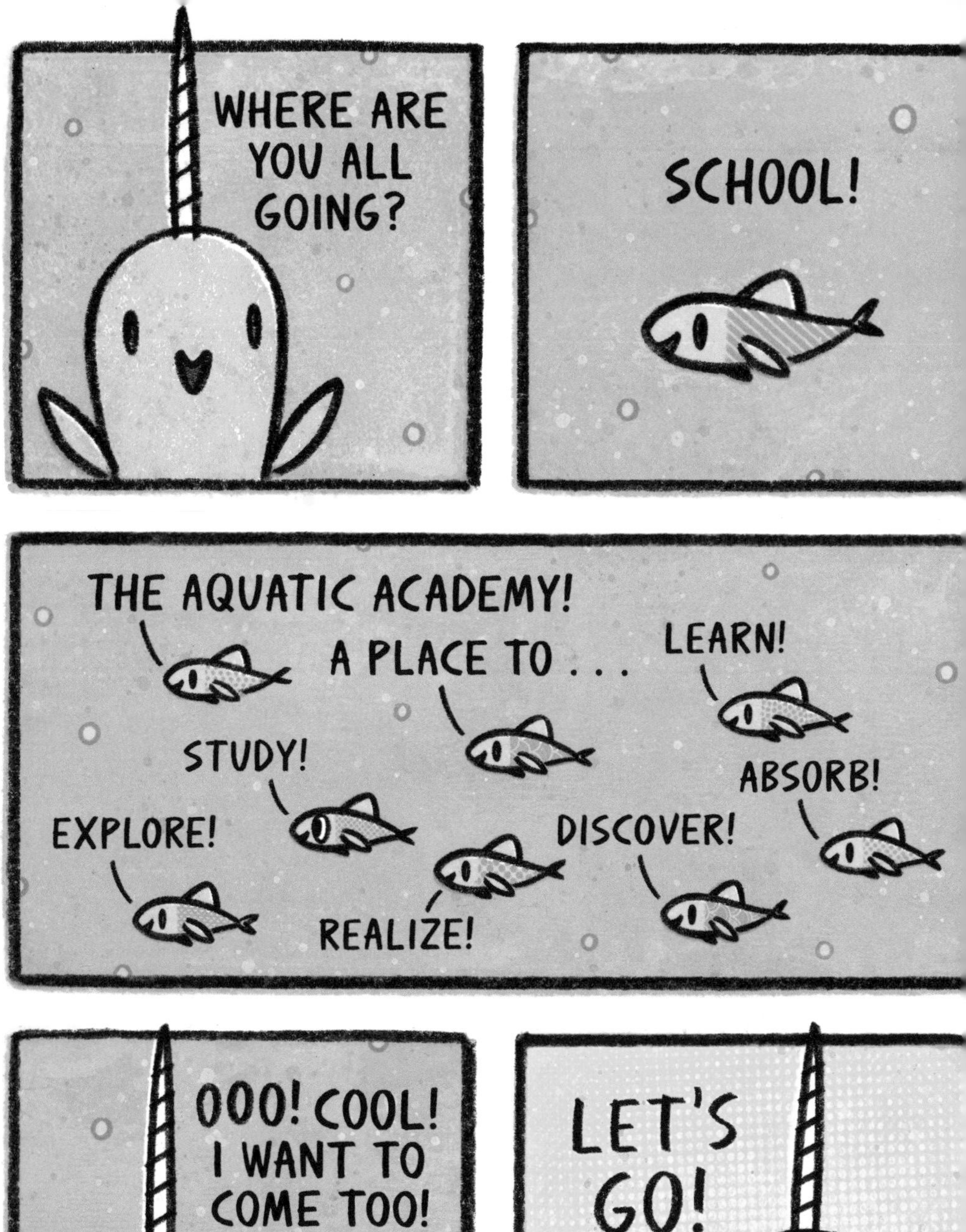
WHERE ARE YOU ALL GOING?
SCHOOL!
THE AQUATIC ACADEMY!
A PLACE TO . . .
LEARN!
STUDY!
ABSORB!
EXPLORE!
DISCOVER!
REALIZE!
OOO! COOL! I WANT TO COME TOO!
LET'S GO!

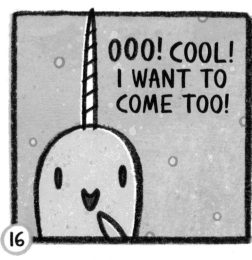

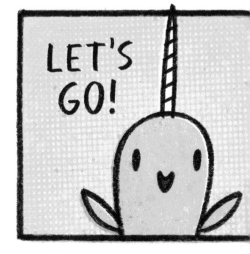

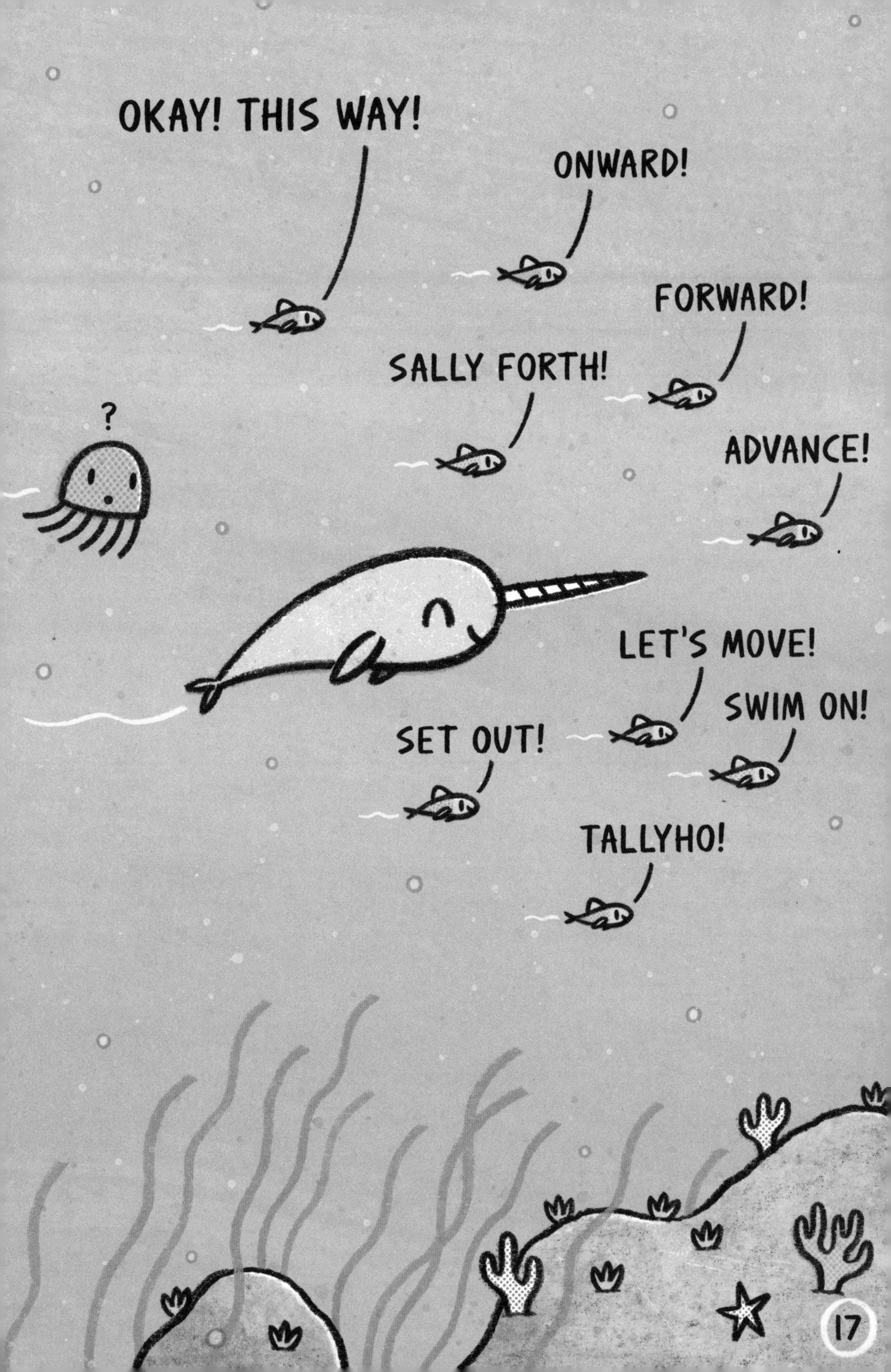

OKAY! THIS WAY!
ONWARD!
FORWARD!
SALLY FORTH!
?
ADVANCE!
LET'S MOVE!
SWIM ON!
SET OUT!
TALLYHO!

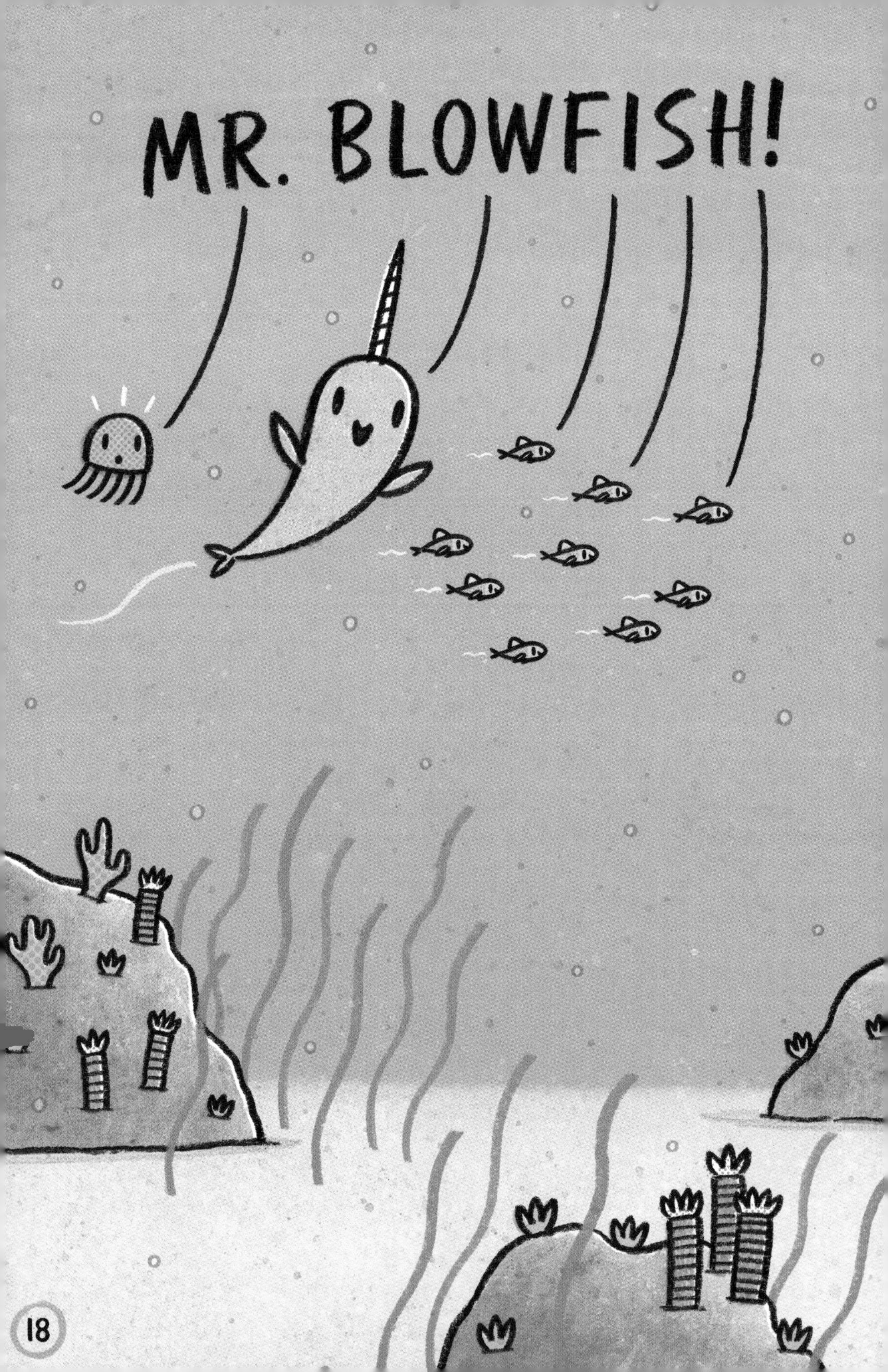
MR. BLOWFISH!

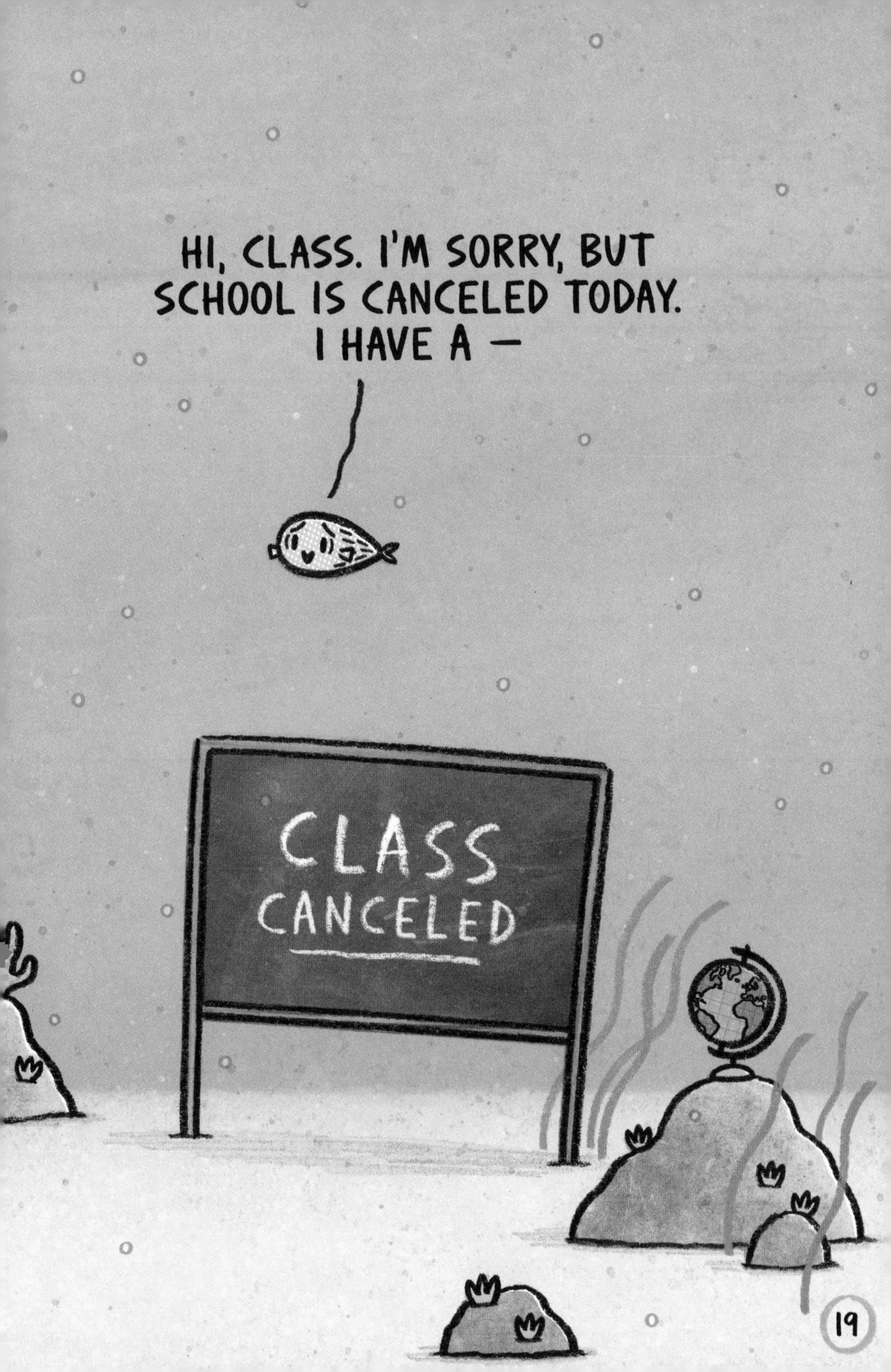
HI, CLASS. I'M SORRY, BUT SCHOOL IS CANCELED TODAY. I HAVE A —
CLASS CANCELED

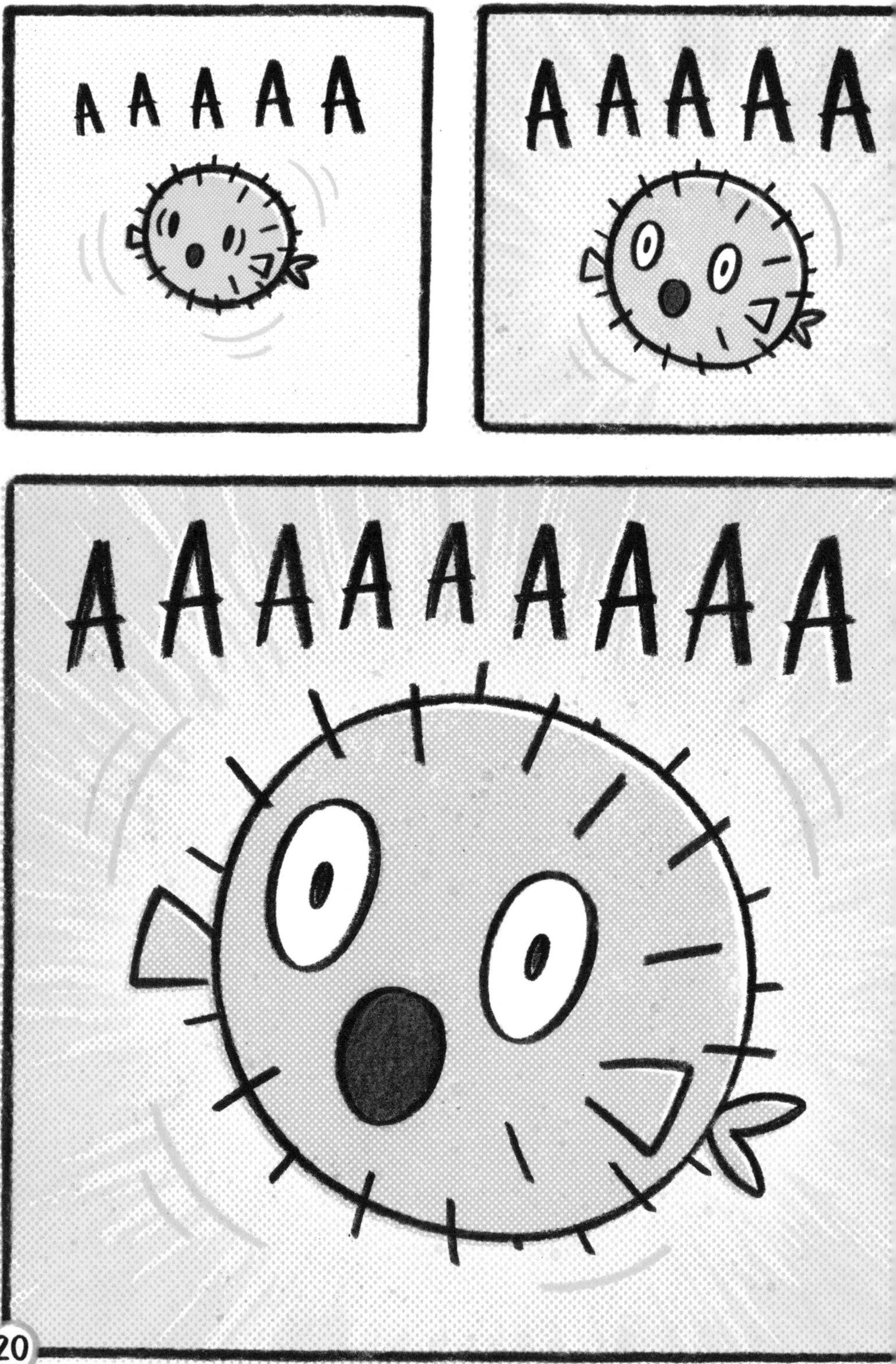
A A A A A
A A A A A
A A A A A A A A A

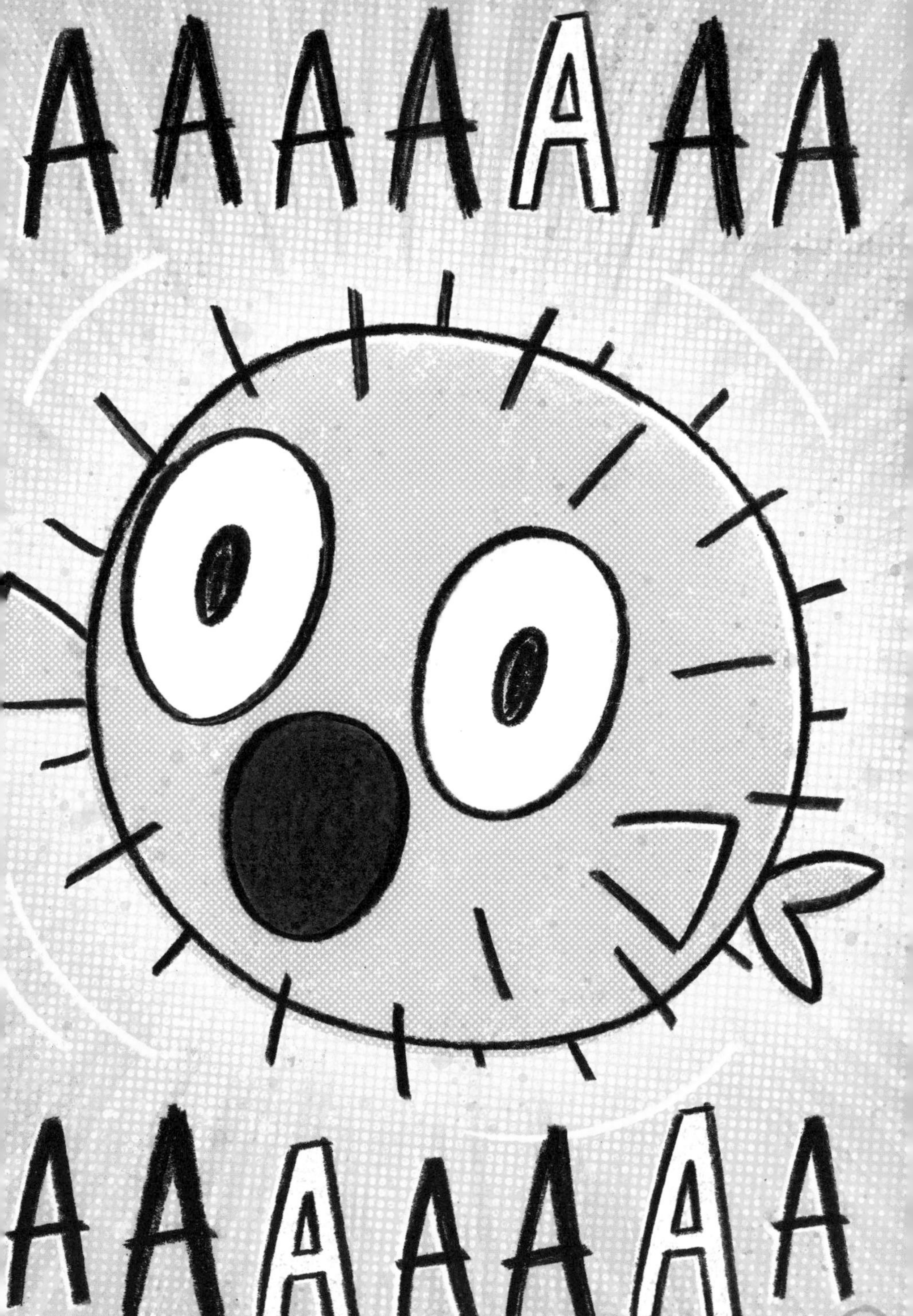
AAAAAAA
AAAAAAA

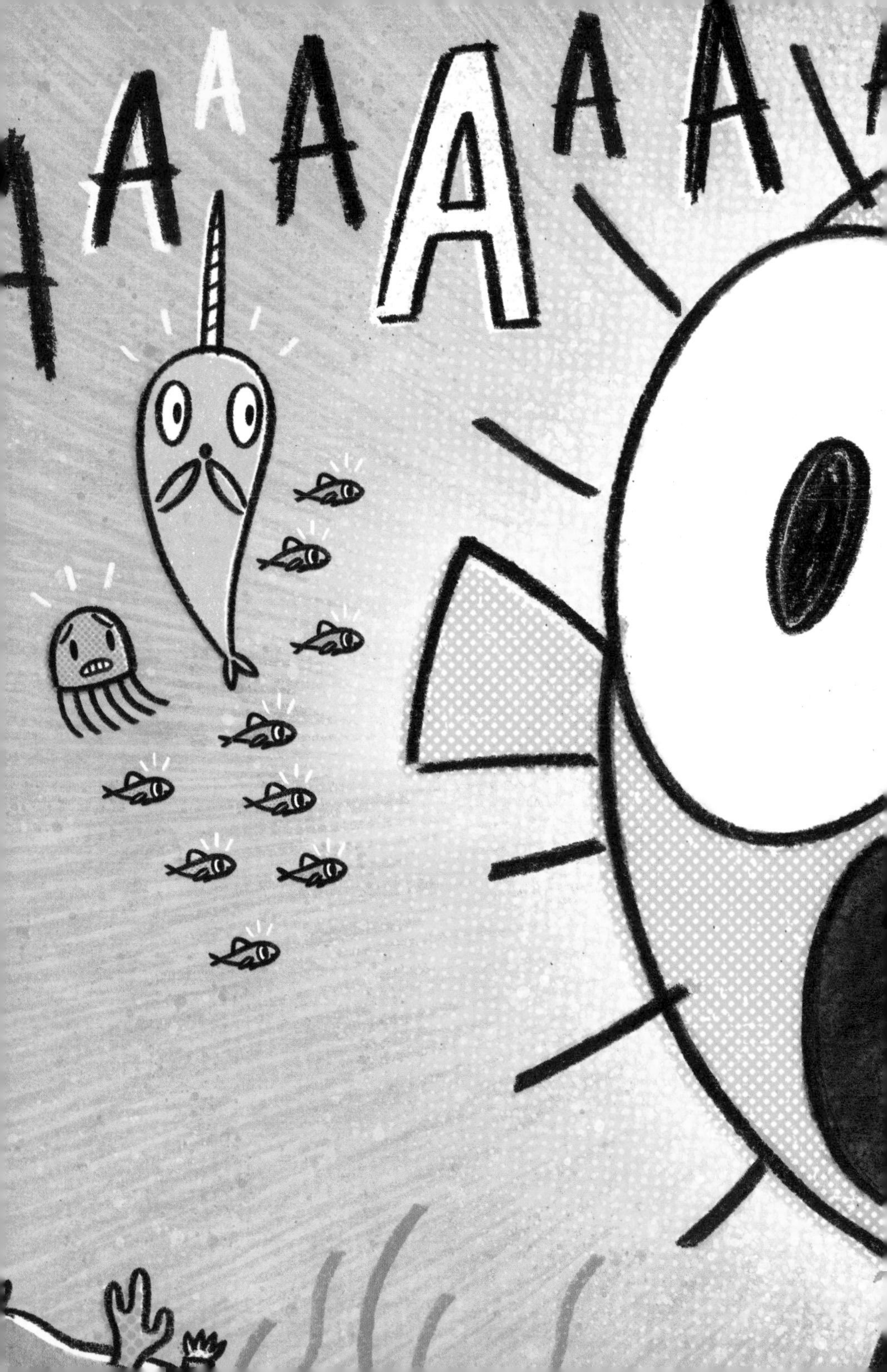
AAAAAA

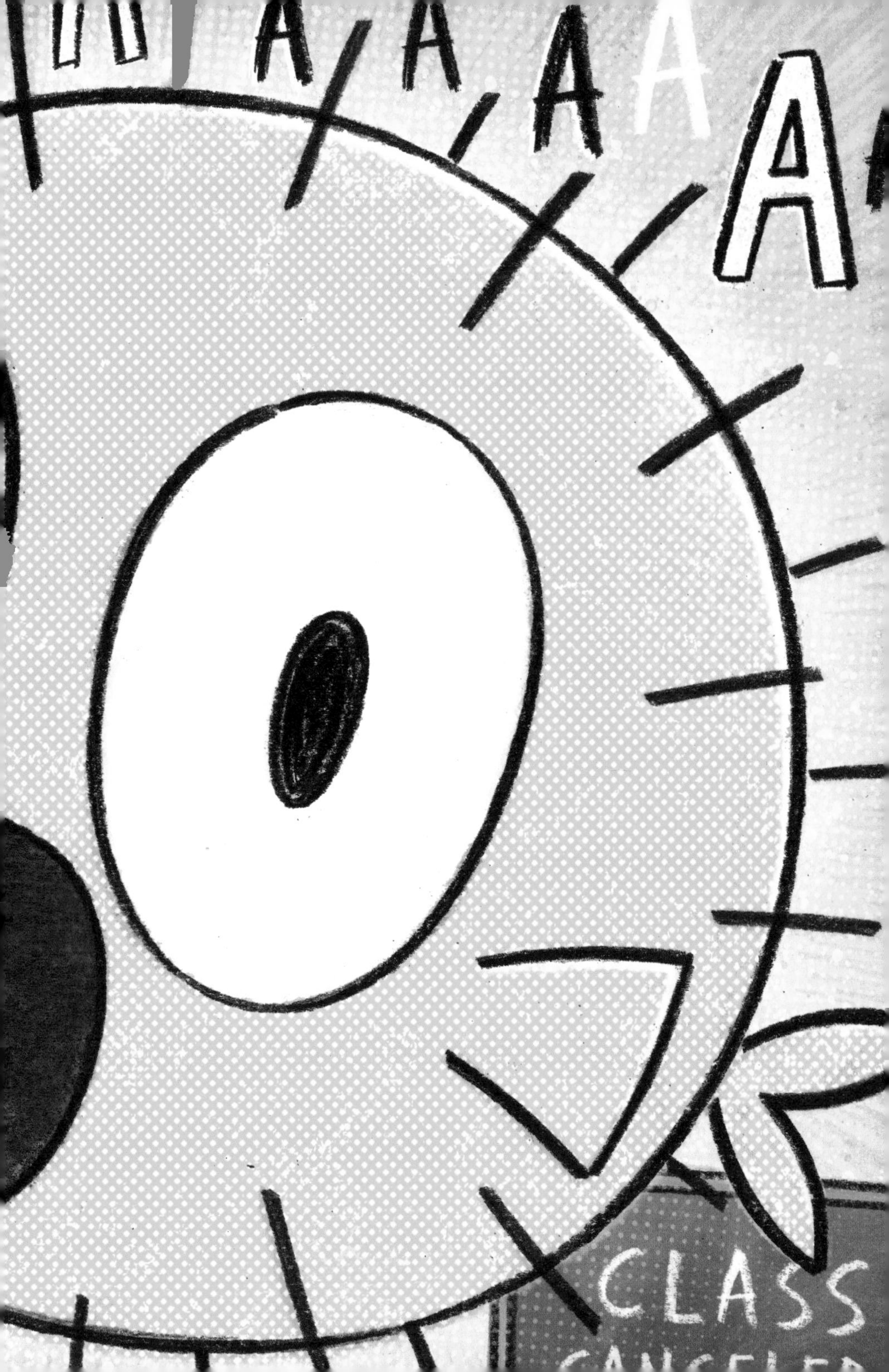
AAAAAA
CLASS

CHOOOOOOOOOOOOOOOOOOOOOOOOOOOOOOO

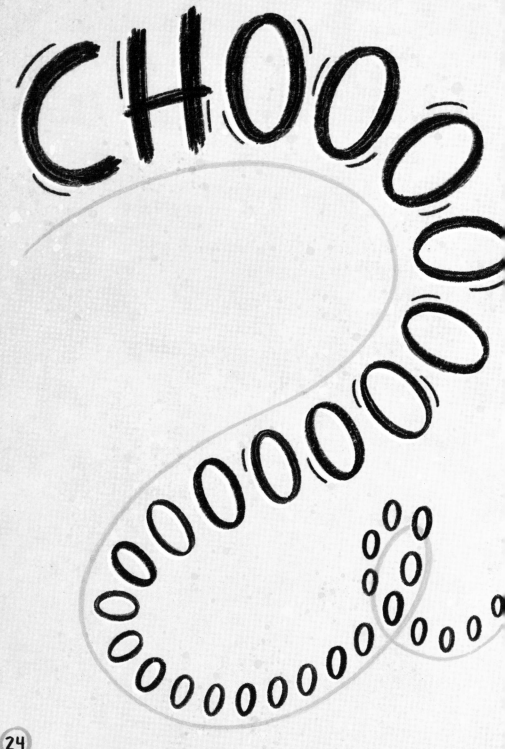

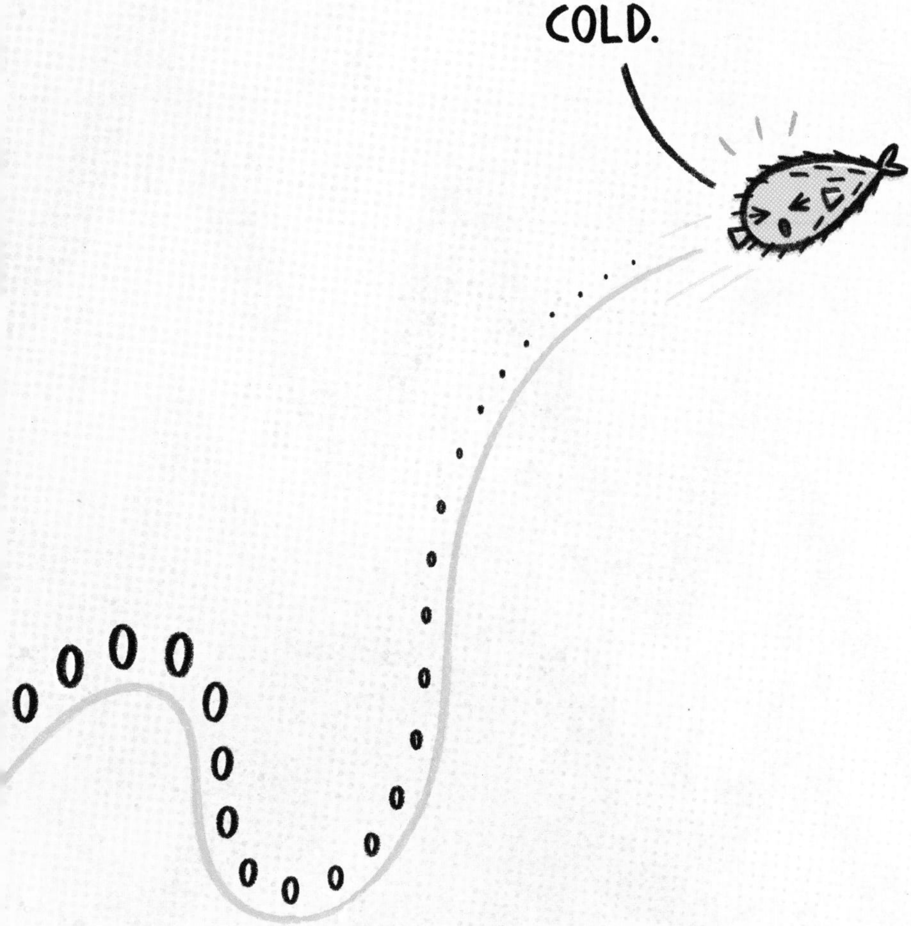
COLD.

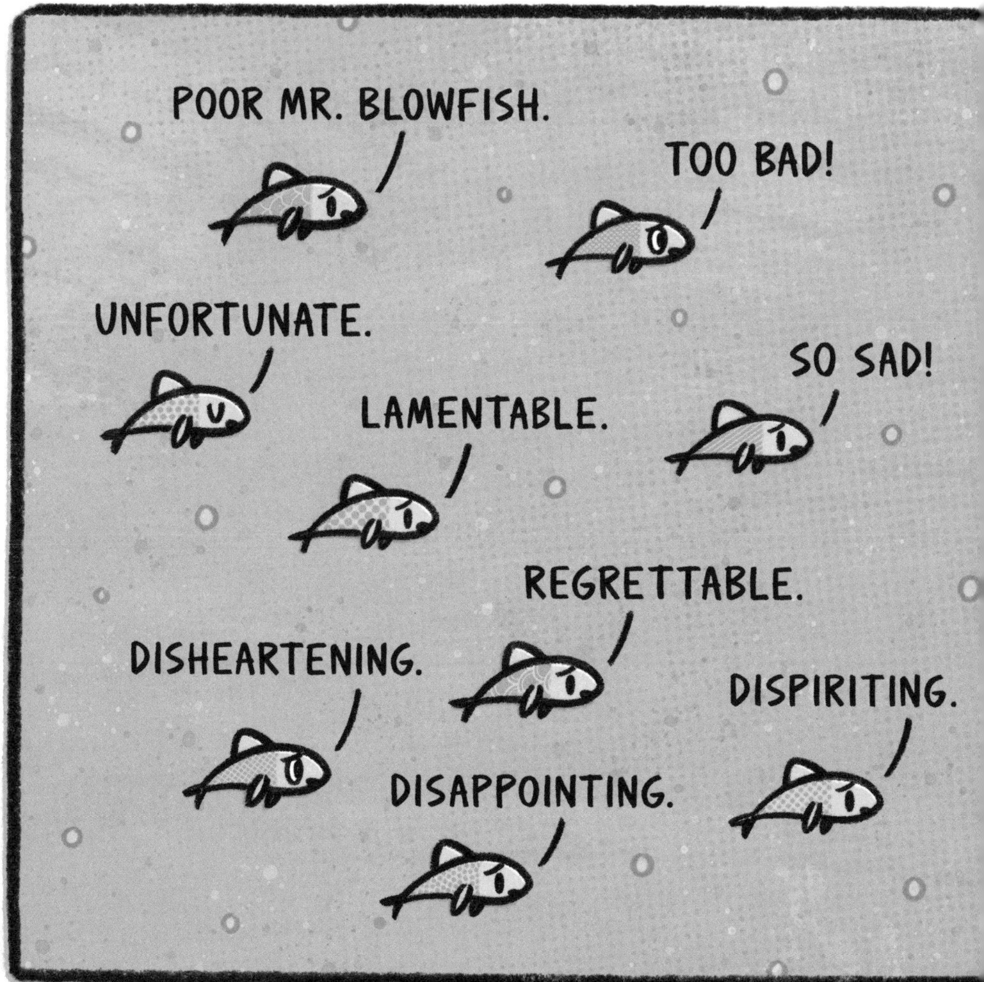
POOR MR. BLOWFISH.
TOO BAD!
UNFORTUNATE.
SO SAD!
LAMENTABLE.
REGRETTABLE.
DISHEARTENING.
DISPIRITING.
DISAPPOINTING.

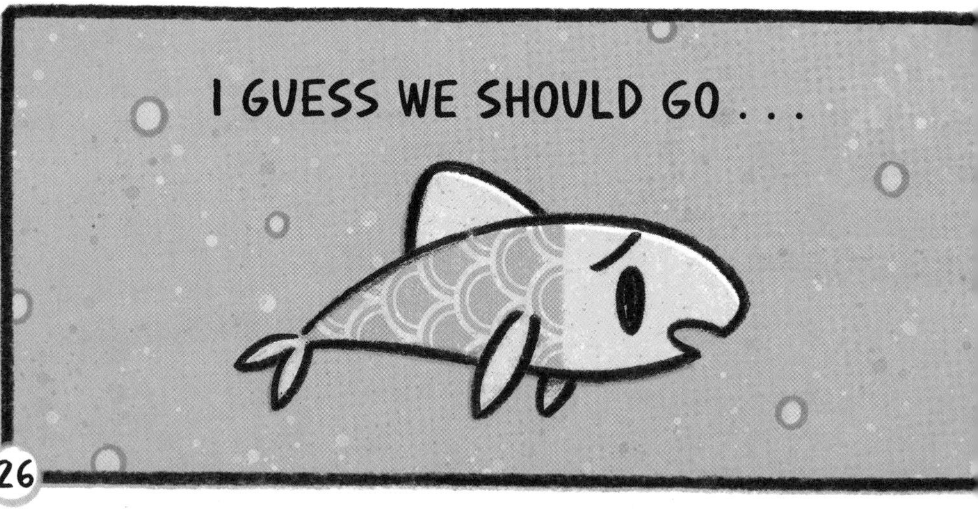
I GUESS WE SHOULD GO . . .

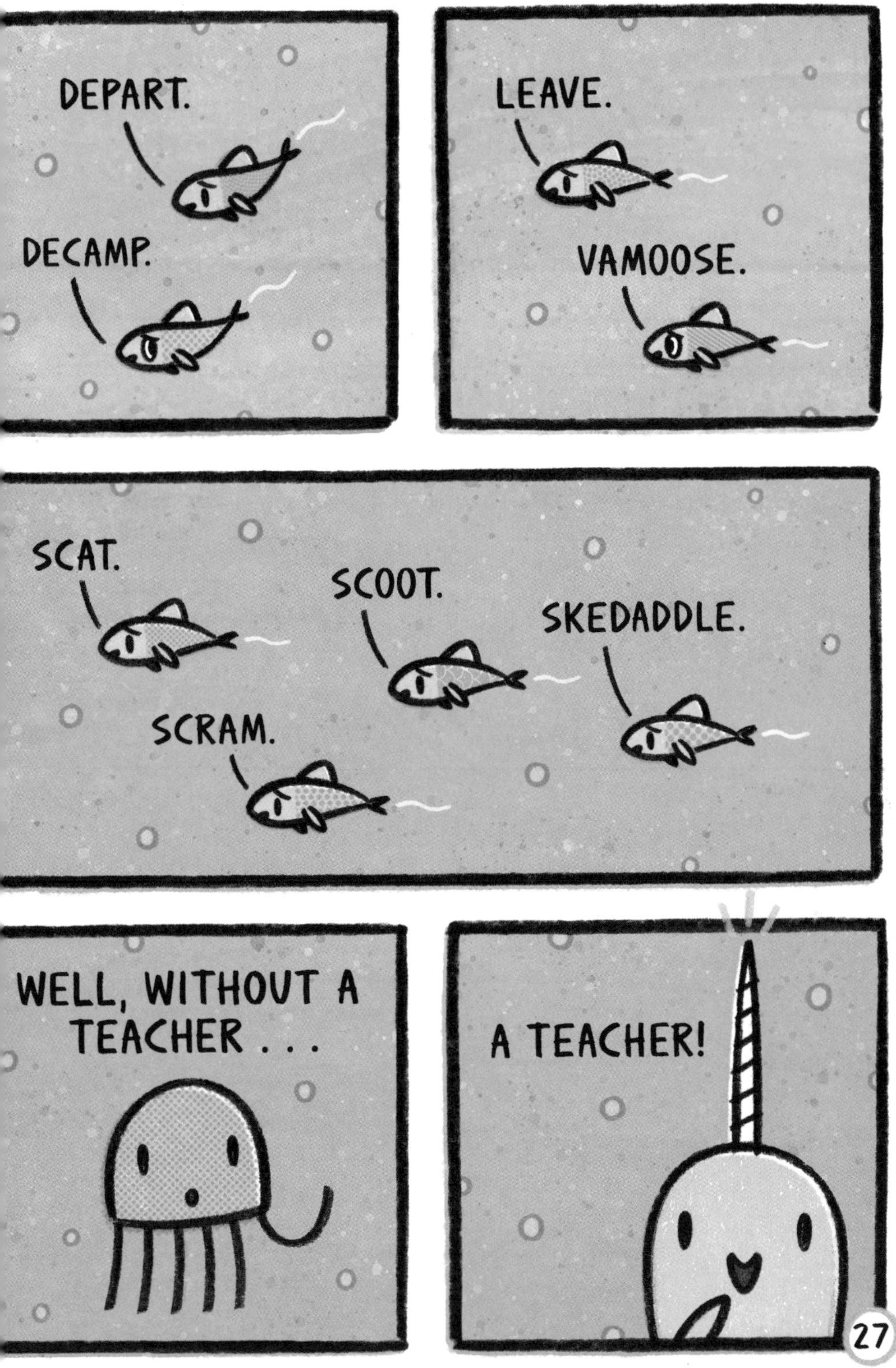
DEPART.
DECAMP.
LEAVE.
VAMOOSE.
SCAT.
SCOOT.
SKEDADDLE.
SCRAM.
WELL, WITHOUT A TEACHER . . .
A TEACHER!

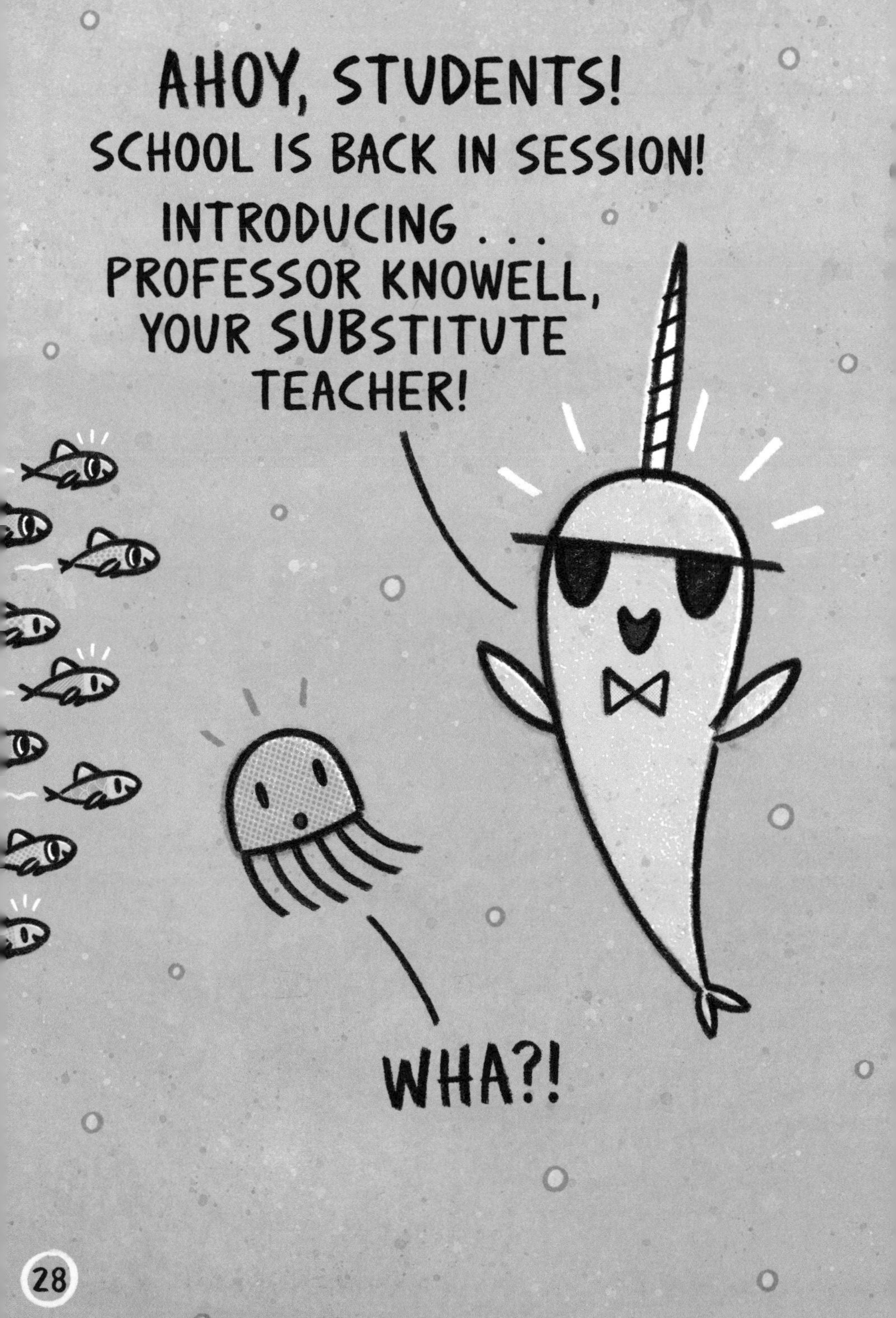
AHOY, STUDENTS!
SCHOOL IS BACK IN SESSION!
INTRODUCING . . .
PROFESSOR KNOWELL,
YOUR SUBSTITUTE
TEACHER!
WHA?!

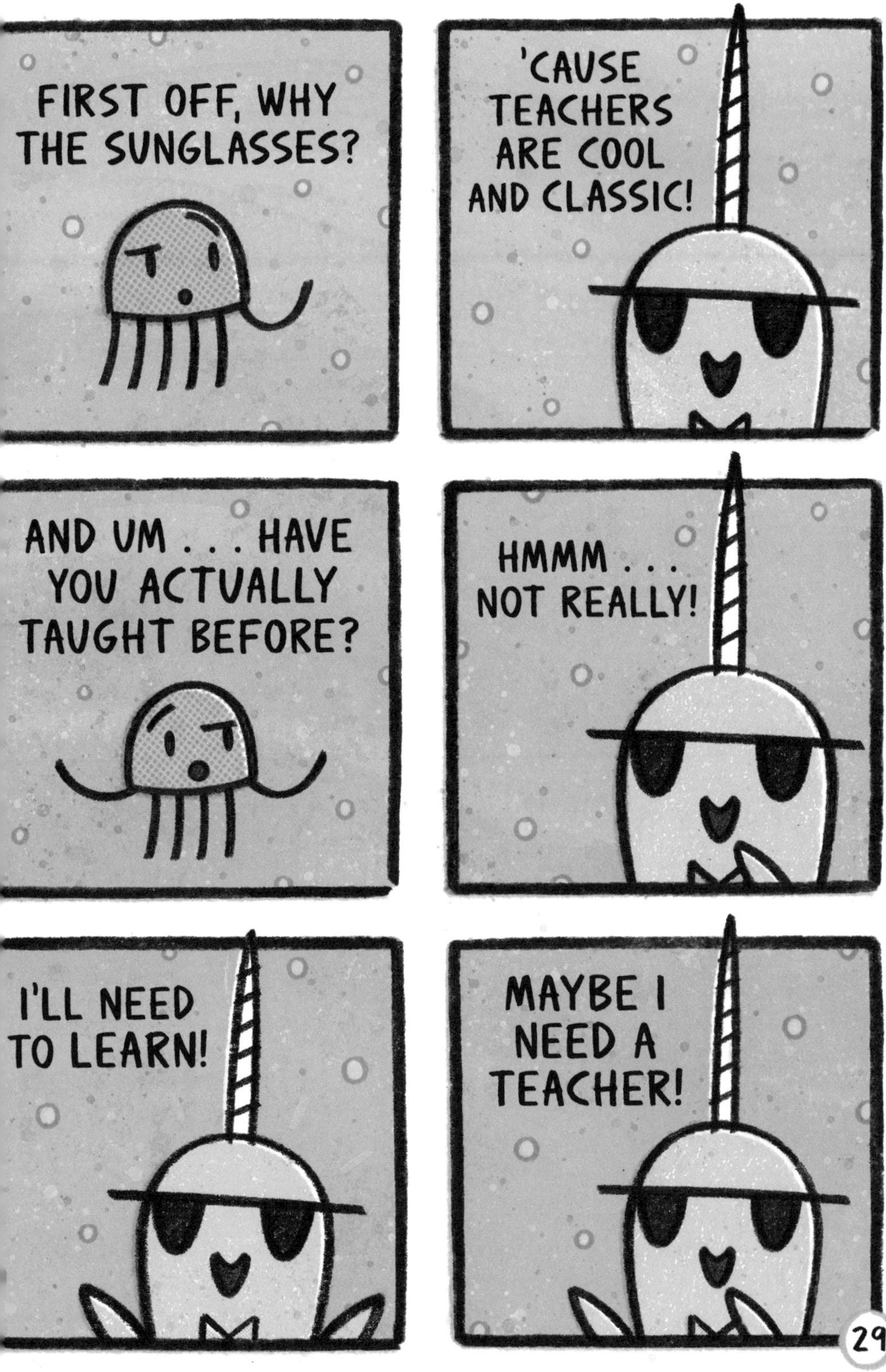
FIRST OFF, WHY THE SUNGLASSES?
'CAUSE TEACHERS ARE COOL AND CLASSIC!
AND UM . . . HAVE YOU ACTUALLY TAUGHT BEFORE?
HMMM . . . NOT REALLY!
I'LL NEED TO LEARN!
MAYBE I NEED A TEACHER!

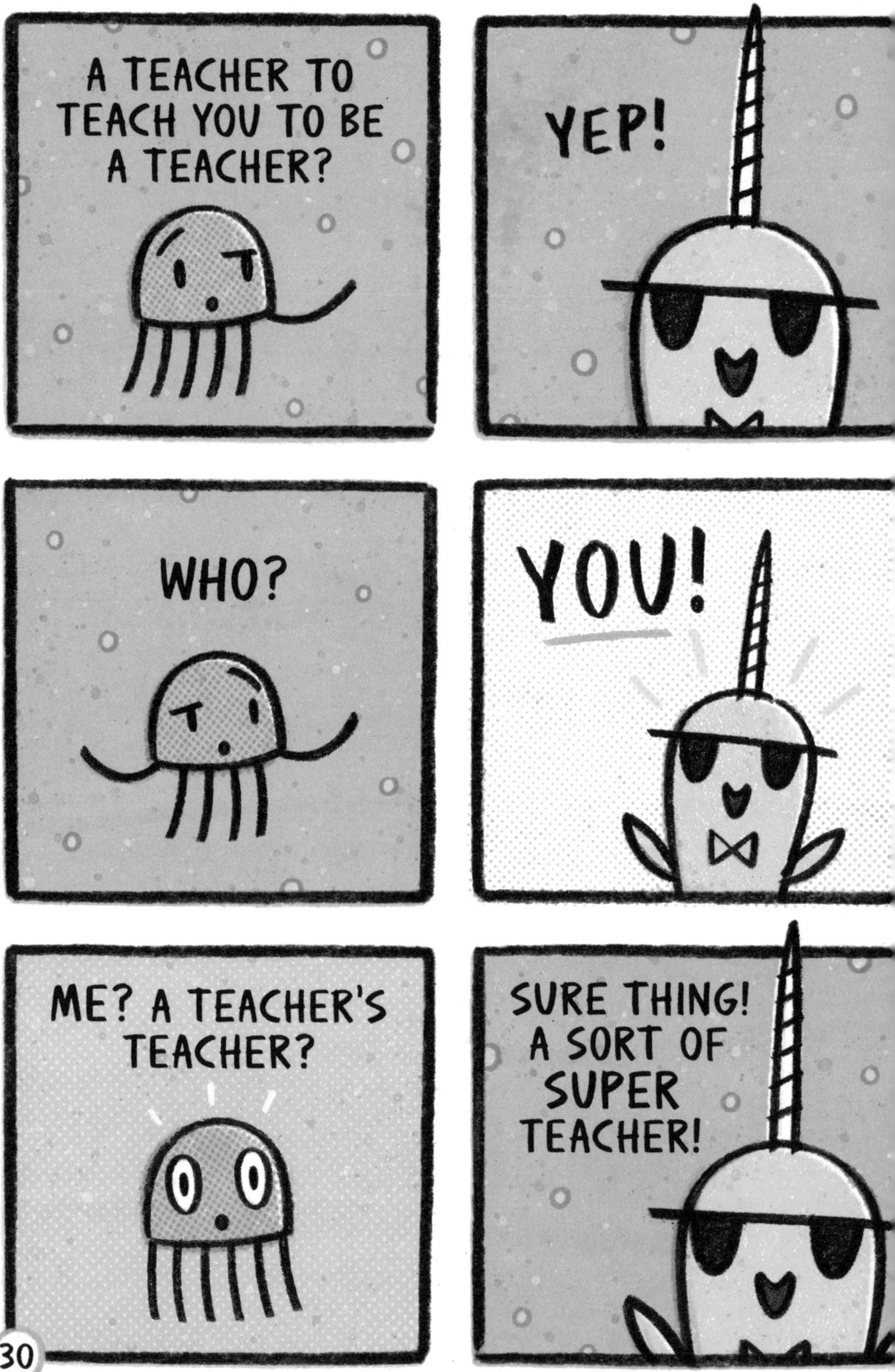
A TEACHER TO TEACH YOU TO BE A TEACHER?
YEP!
WHO?
YOU!
ME? A TEACHER'S TEACHER?
SURE THING! A SORT OF SUPER TEACHER!

A SUPER TEACHER?

PRETTY MUCH!

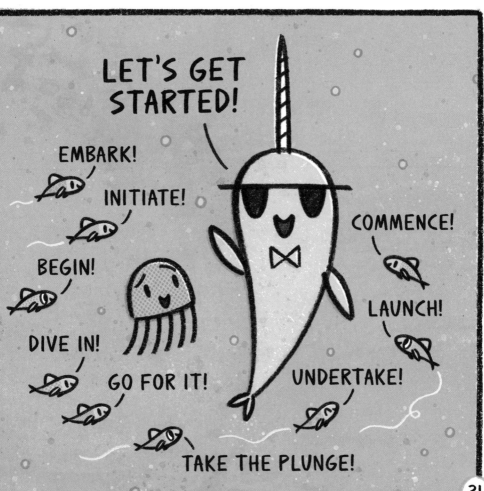

LET'S GET STARTED!

EMBARK!

INITIATE!

BEGIN!

DIVE IN!

GO FOR IT!

COMMENCE!

LAUNCH!

UNDERTAKE!

TAKE THE PLUNGE!

THIS IS GOING TO BE
FINTASTIC!

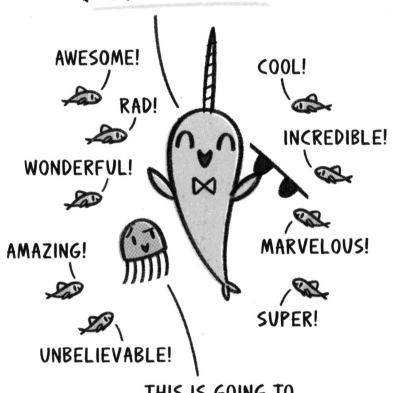

AWESOME!

COOL!

RAD!

INCREDIBLE!

WONDERFUL!

AMAZING!

MARVELOUS!

SUPER!

UNBELIEVABLE!

THIS IS GOING TO
BE . . . SOMETHING.

A GREAT GROUP OF FUN FACTS

YOU PROBABLY ALREADY KNOW THAT A GROUP OF CHICKENS IS CALLED A FLOCK AND A GROUP OF DEER IS COMMONLY CALLED A HERD. BUT HAVE YOU HEARD OF A TOWER OF GIRAFFES OR A BLOAT OF HIPPOS? MANY SEA CREATURES HAVE FUN GROUP NAMES TOO!

NEAT!

FASCINATING!

CAPTIVATING!

INTERESTING!

A GROUP OF FISH ALL THE SAME SPECIES AND SWIMMING IN SYNC IS KNOWN AS A SCHOOL. THE SIZE AND SYNCHRONIZED MOVEMENTS OF A SCHOOL OF FISH CAN CONFUSE AND EVEN SCARE PREDATORS.

EEP! MONSTER!

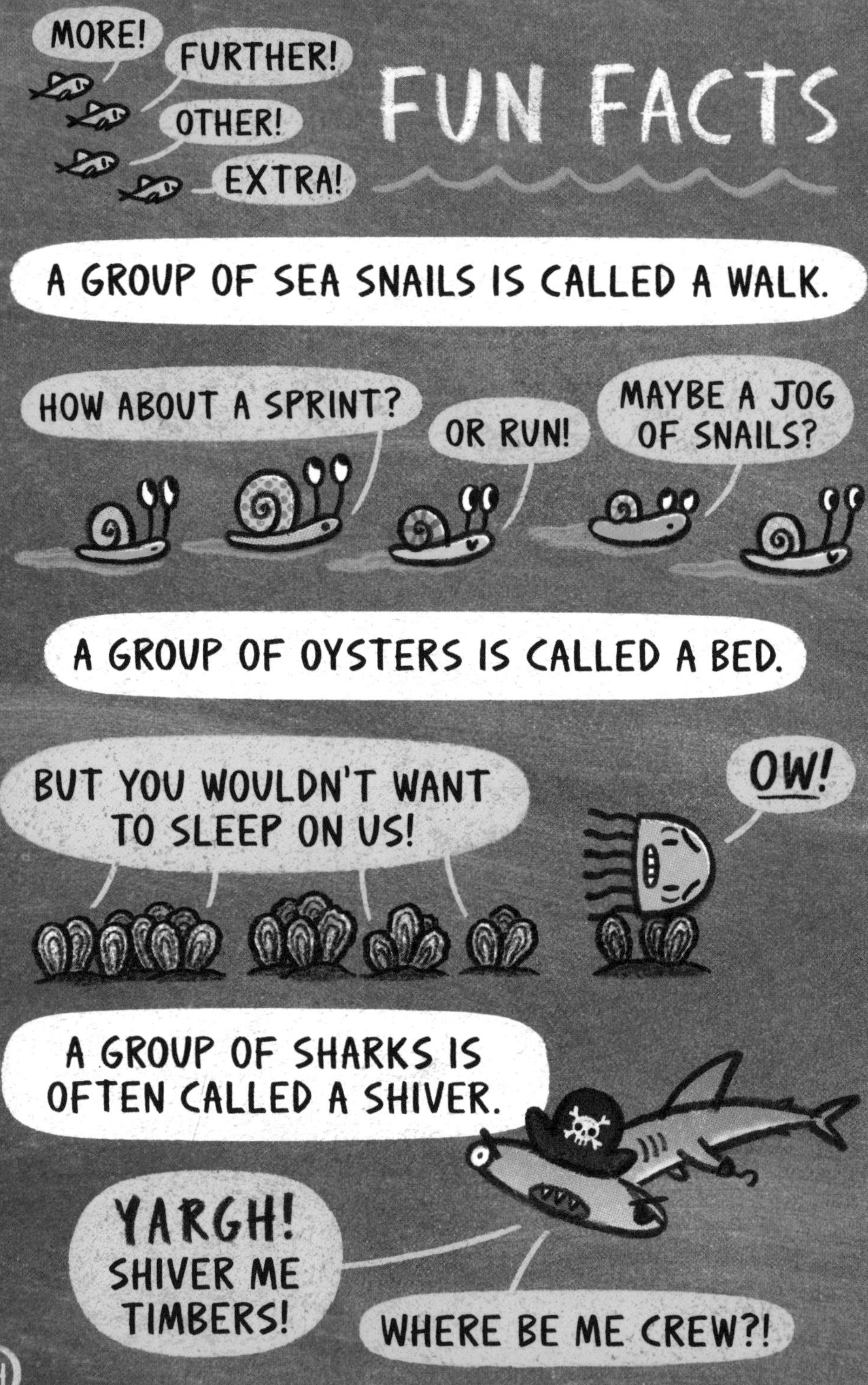
MORE!
FURTHER!
OTHER!
EXTRA!
FUN FACTS
A GROUP OF SEA SNAILS IS CALLED A WALK.
HOW ABOUT A SPRINT?
OR RUN!
MAYBE A JOG OF SNAILS?
A GROUP OF OYSTERS IS CALLED A BED.
BUT YOU WOULDN'T WANT TO SLEEP ON US!
OW!
A GROUP OF SHARKS IS OFTEN CALLED A SHIVER.
YARGH! SHIVER ME TIMBERS!
WHERE BE ME CREW?!

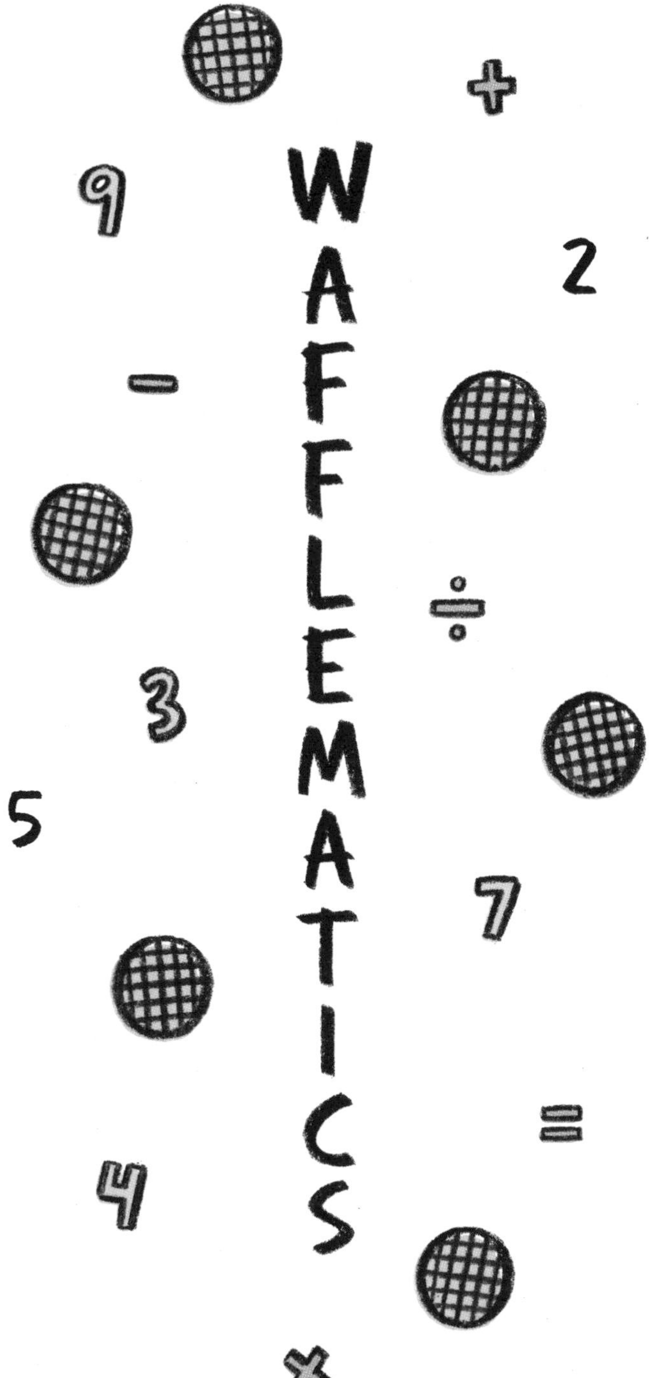
WAFFLEMATICS
+
9
2
−
÷
3
5
7
=
4
×

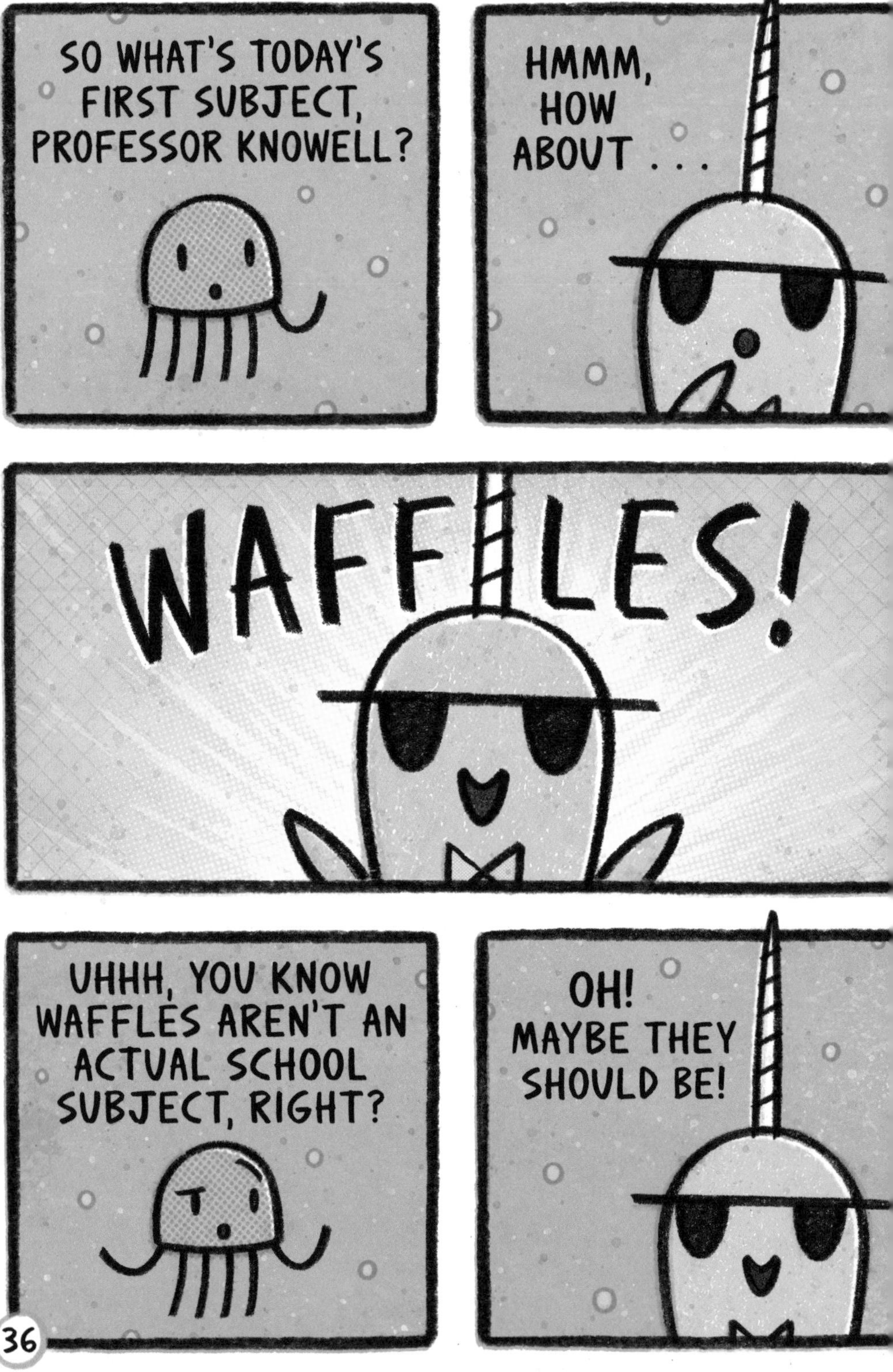
SO WHAT'S TODAY'S FIRST SUBJECT, PROFESSOR KNOWELL?
HMMM, HOW ABOUT . . .
WAFFLES!
UHHH, YOU KNOW WAFFLES AREN'T AN ACTUAL SCHOOL SUBJECT, RIGHT?
OH! MAYBE THEY SHOULD BE!

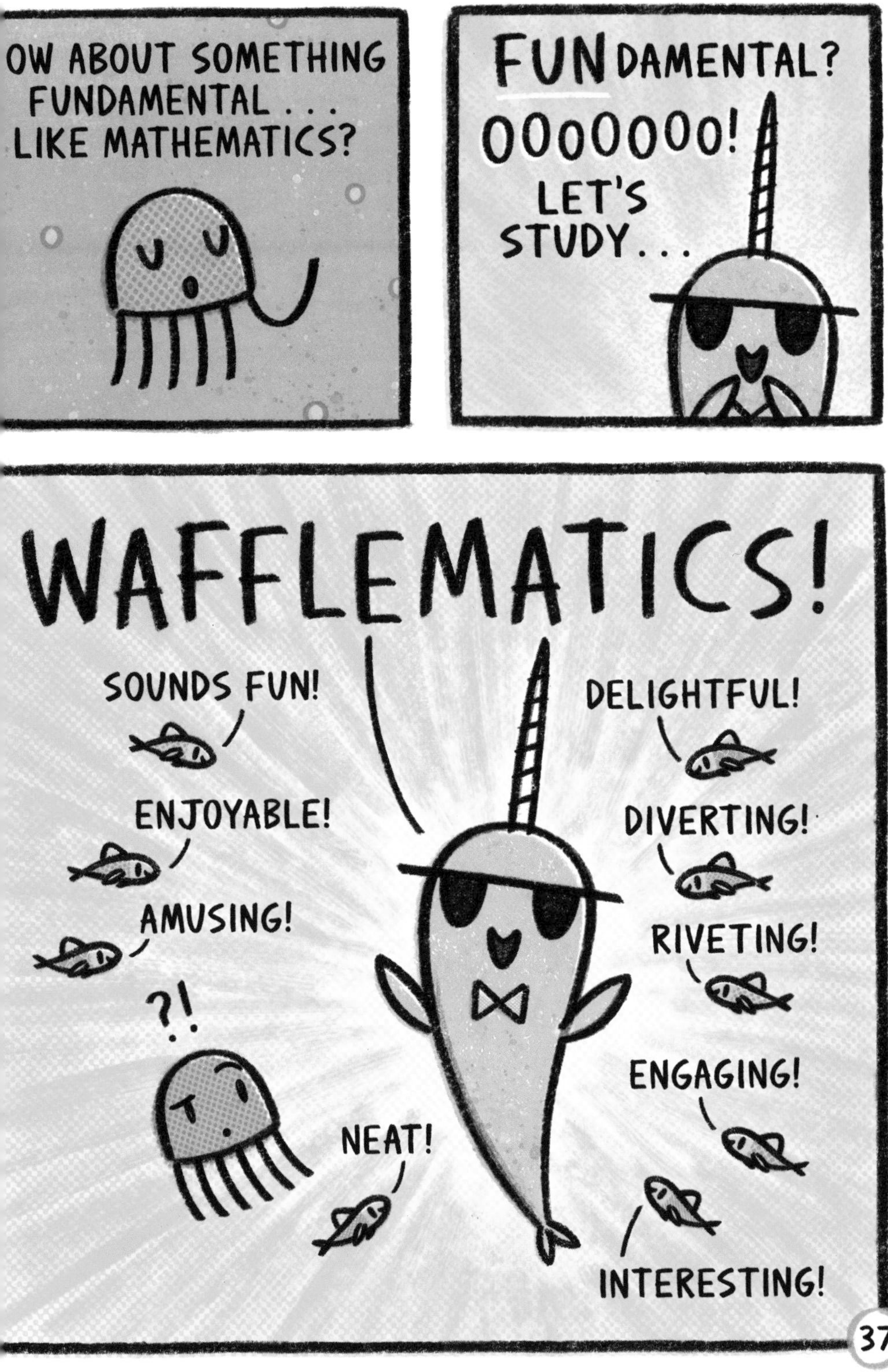
OW ABOUT SOMETHING FUNDAMENTAL . . . LIKE MATHEMATICS?
FUNDAMENTAL?
OOOOOOO! LET'S STUDY . . .
WAFFLEMATICS!
SOUNDS FUN!
ENJOYABLE!
AMUSING!
?!
NEAT!
DELIGHTFUL!
DIVERTING!
RIVETING!
ENGAGING!
INTERESTING!

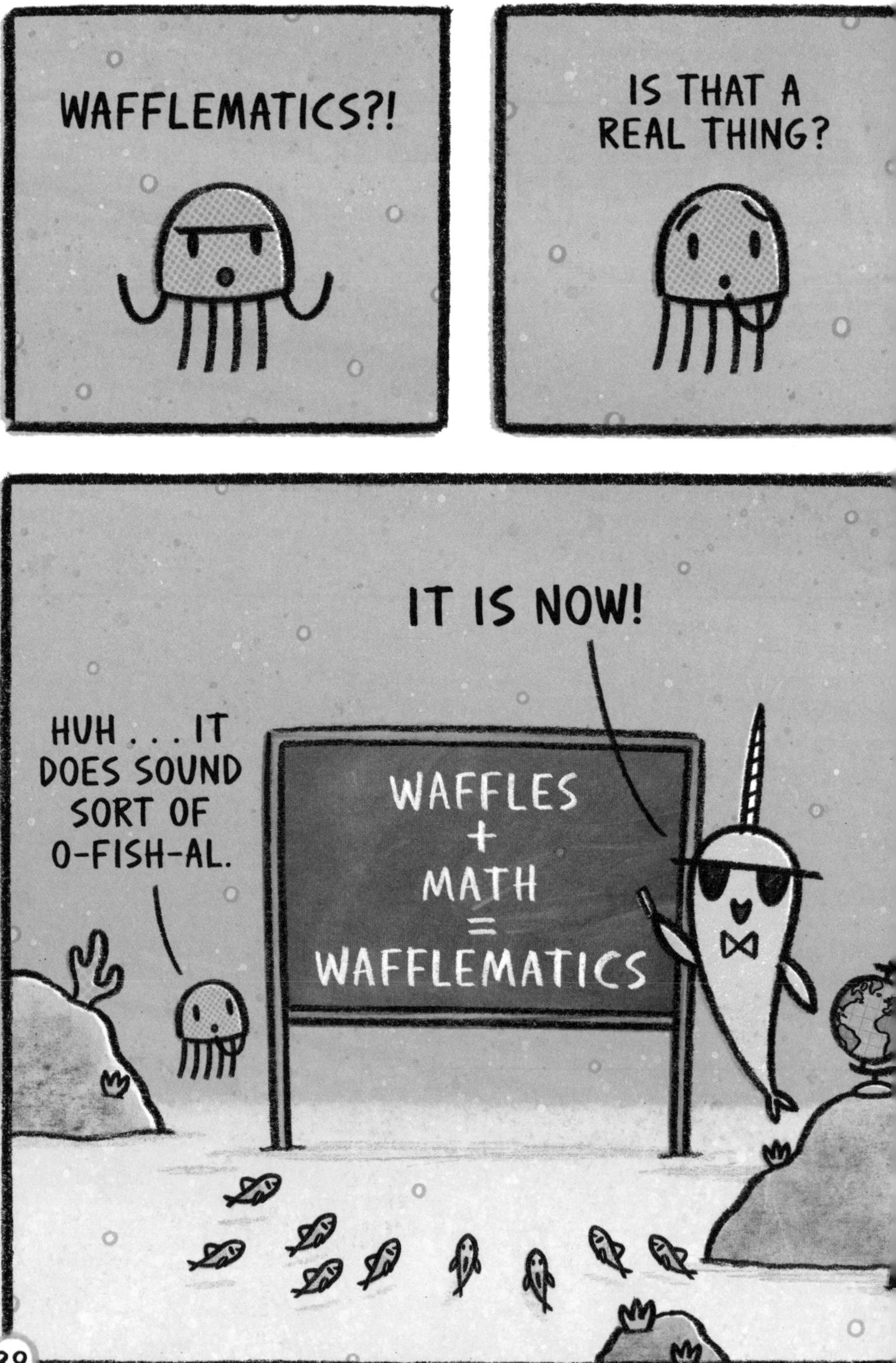
WAFFLEMATICS?!
IS THAT A REAL THING?
IT IS NOW!
HUH . . . IT DOES SOUND SORT OF O-FISH-AL.
WAFFLES + MATH = WAFFLEMATICS

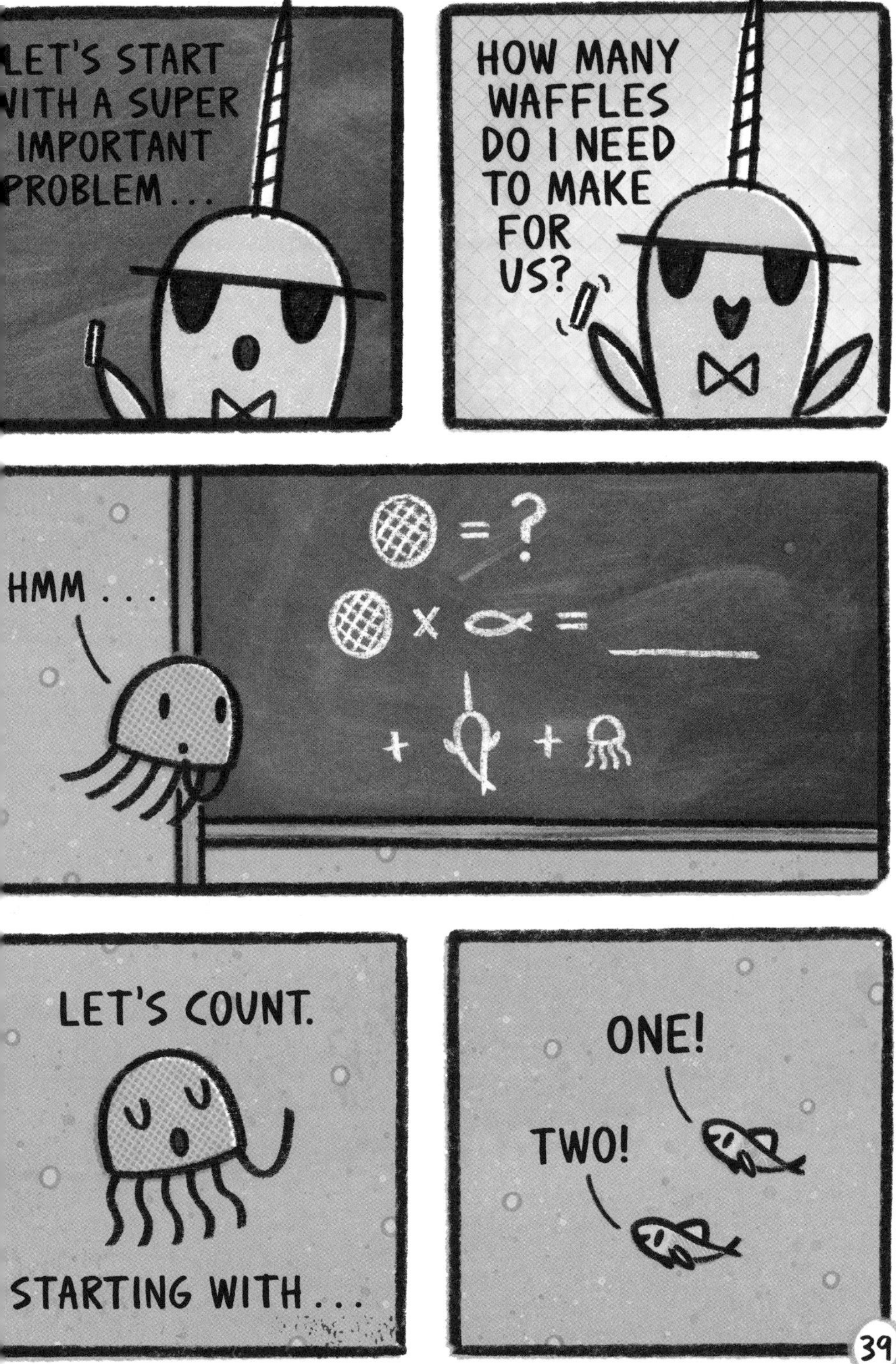
LET'S START WITH A SUPER IMPORTANT PROBLEM...
HOW MANY WAFFLES DO I NEED TO MAKE FOR US?
HMM...
LET'S COUNT.
STARTING WITH...
ONE!
TWO!

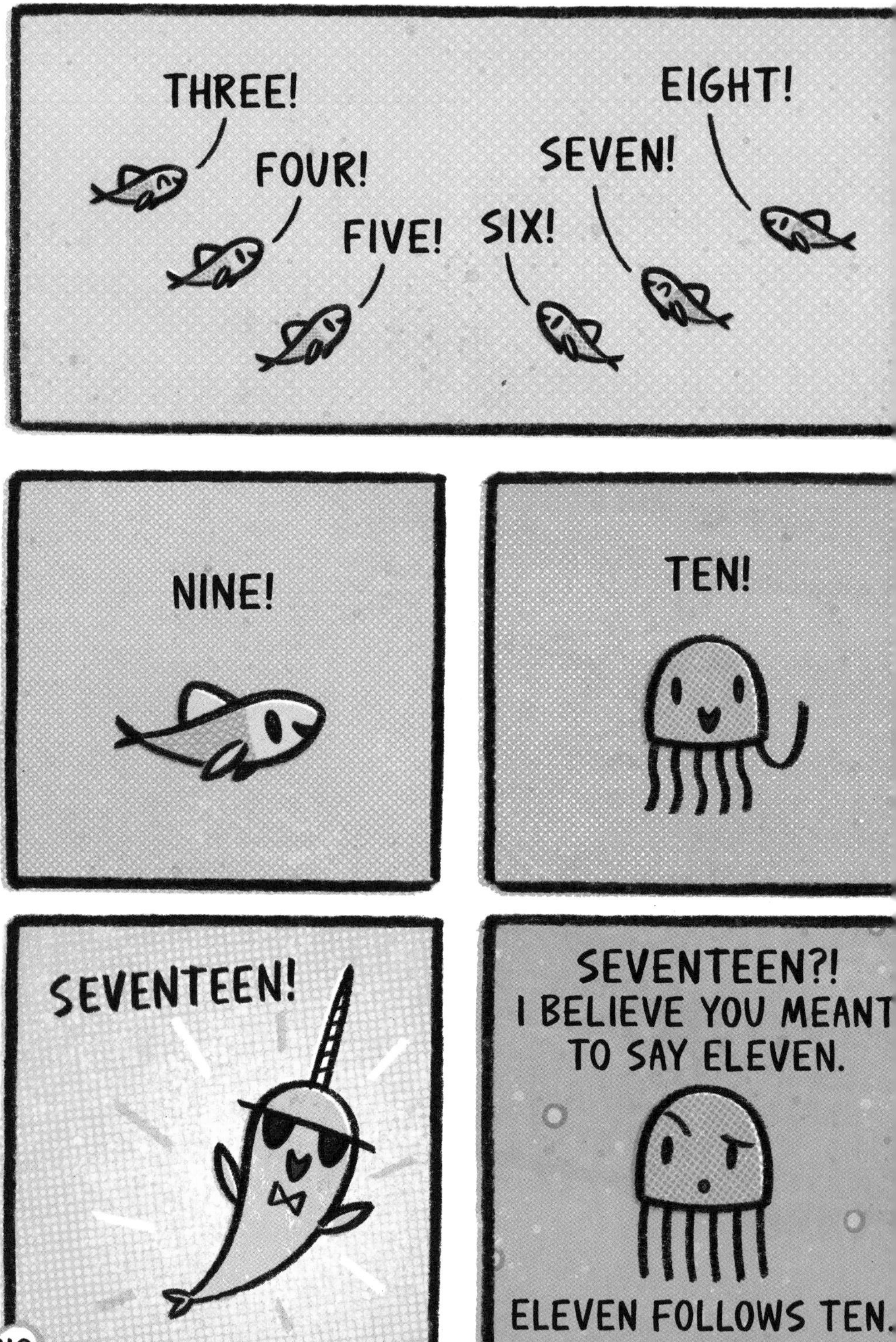
THREE!
FOUR!
FIVE!
SIX!
SEVEN!
EIGHT!
NINE!
TEN!
SEVENTEEN!
SEVENTEEN?! I BELIEVE YOU MEANT TO SAY ELEVEN.
ELEVEN FOLLOWS TEN.

TRUE!
BUT I WANT
TO EAT AT
LEAST SEVEN
WAFFLES!

OH! I'D LIKE
TWO ACTUALLY!

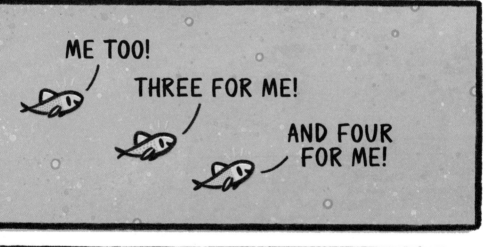

ME TOO!

THREE FOR ME!

AND FOUR
FOR ME!

THIS IS WHAT I'M CHALKING
ABOUT! THIS IS ADDING UP
TO OODLES OF WAFFLES!

7 + 2 + 2 + 3 + 4

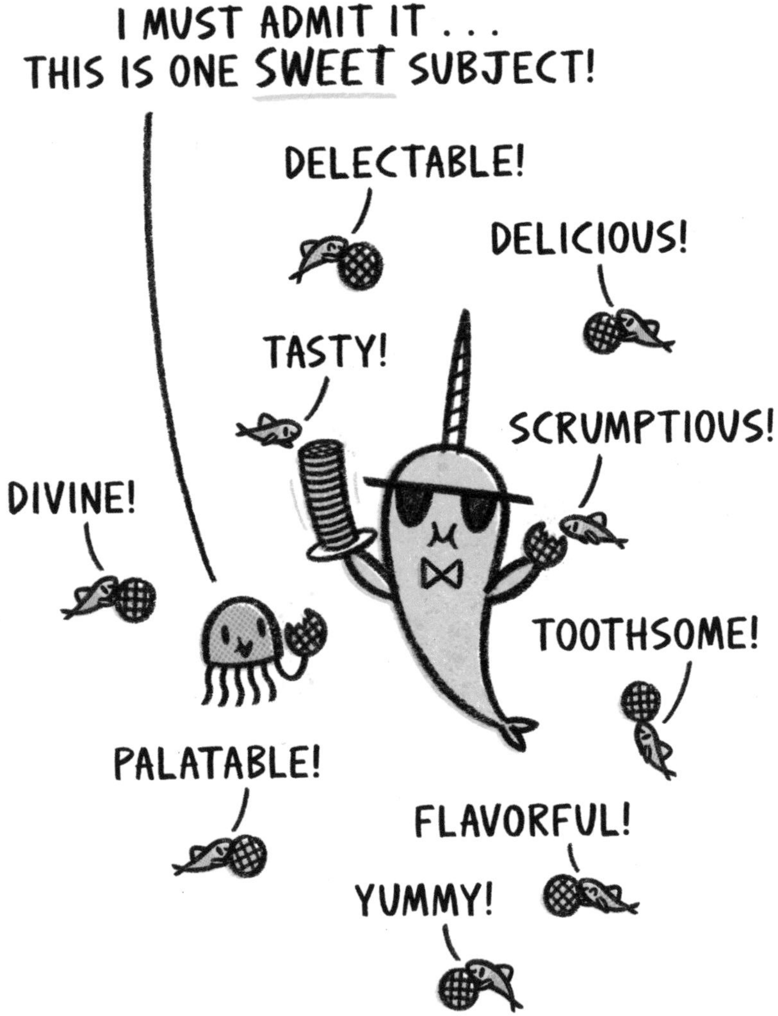

I MUST ADMIT IT . . .
THIS IS ONE SWEET SUBJECT!
DELECTABLE!
DELICIOUS!
TASTY!
SCRUMPTIOUS!
DIVINE!
TOOTHSOME!
PALATABLE!
FLAVORFUL!
YUMMY!

SCIENCE SQUAD

VS.

FUN FINDERS

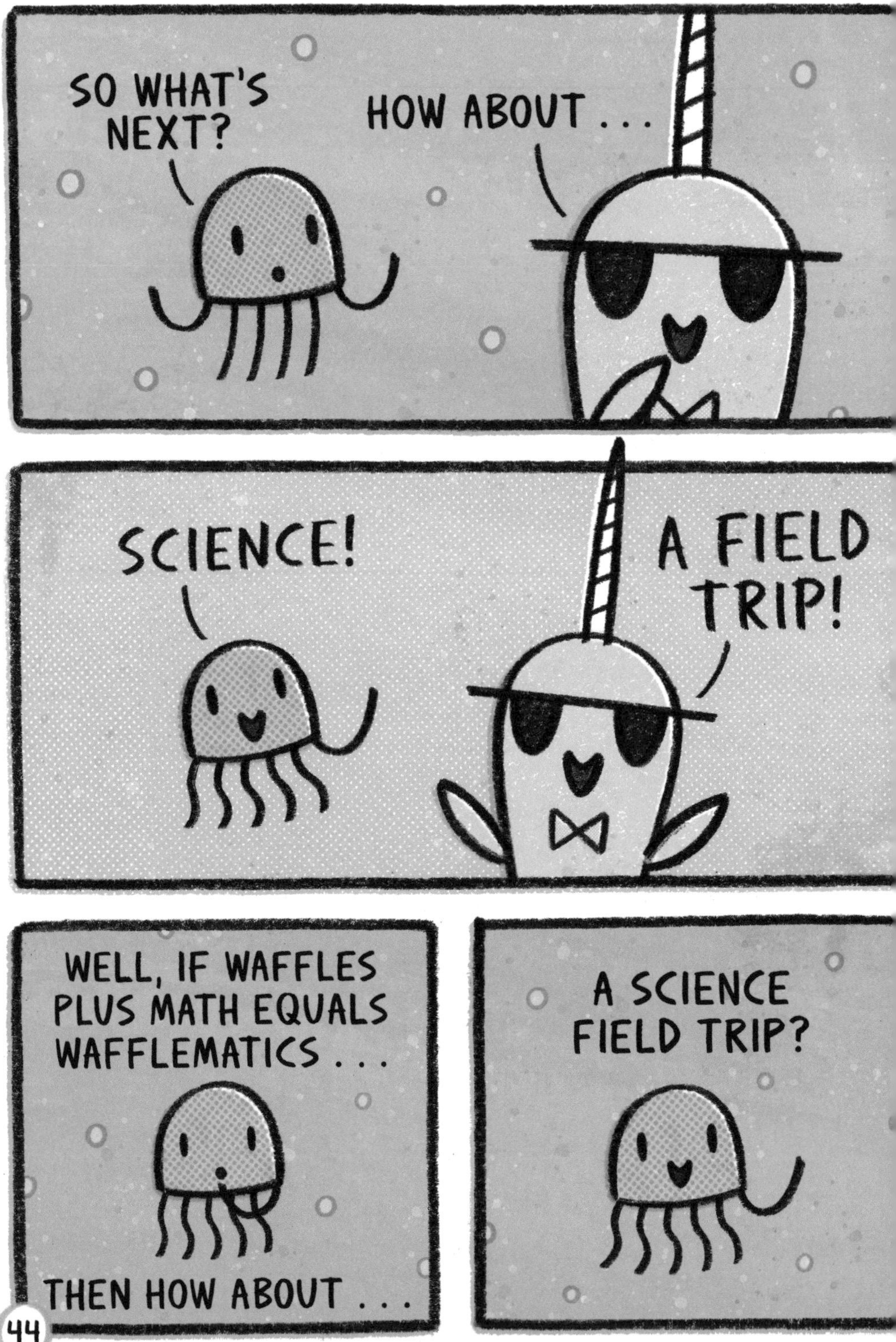

SO WHAT'S NEXT?
HOW ABOUT . . .
SCIENCE!
A FIELD TRIP!
WELL, IF WAFFLES PLUS MATH EQUALS WAFFLEMATICS . . .
THEN HOW ABOUT . . .
A SCIENCE FIELD TRIP?

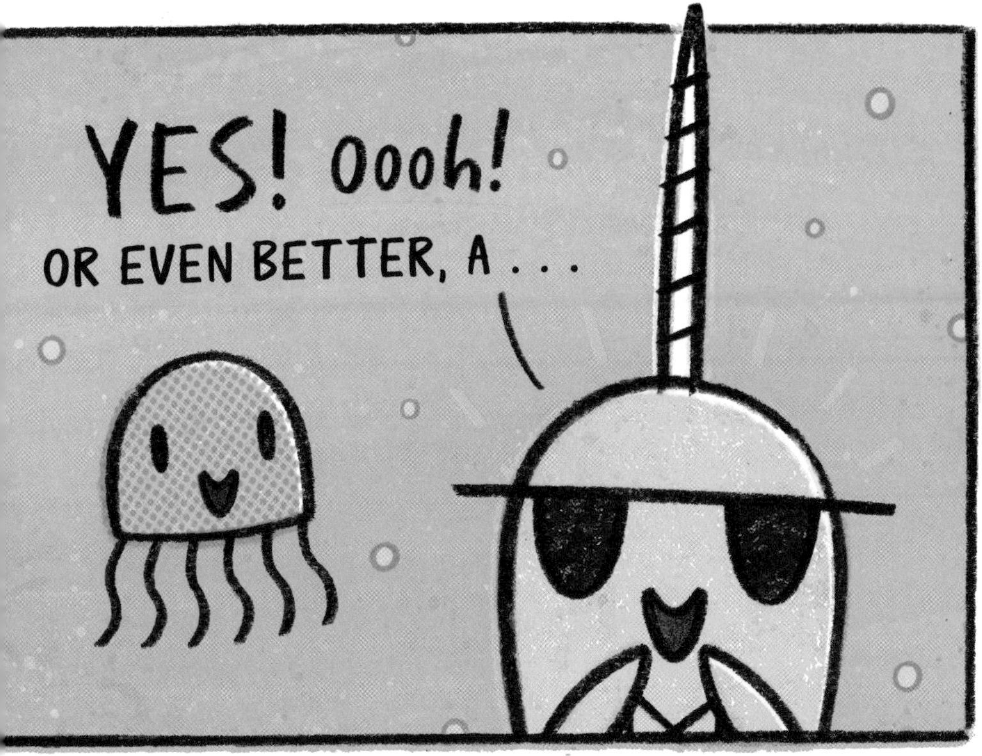
YES! Oooh!
OR EVEN BETTER, A . . .

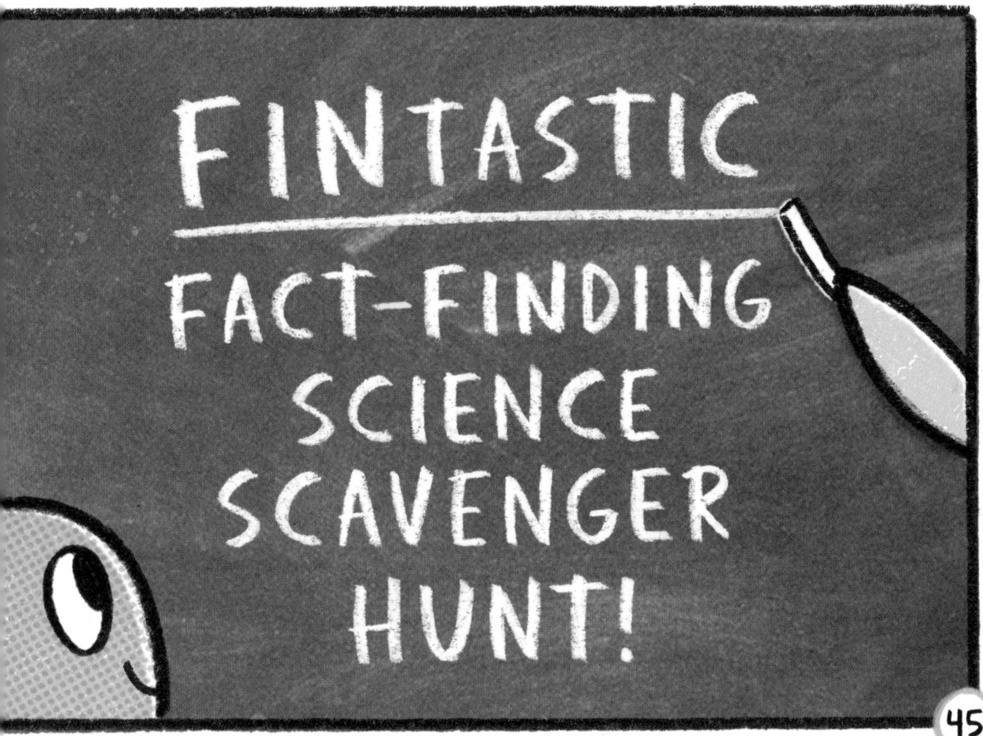
FINTASTIC
FACT-FINDING SCIENCE SCAVENGER HUNT!

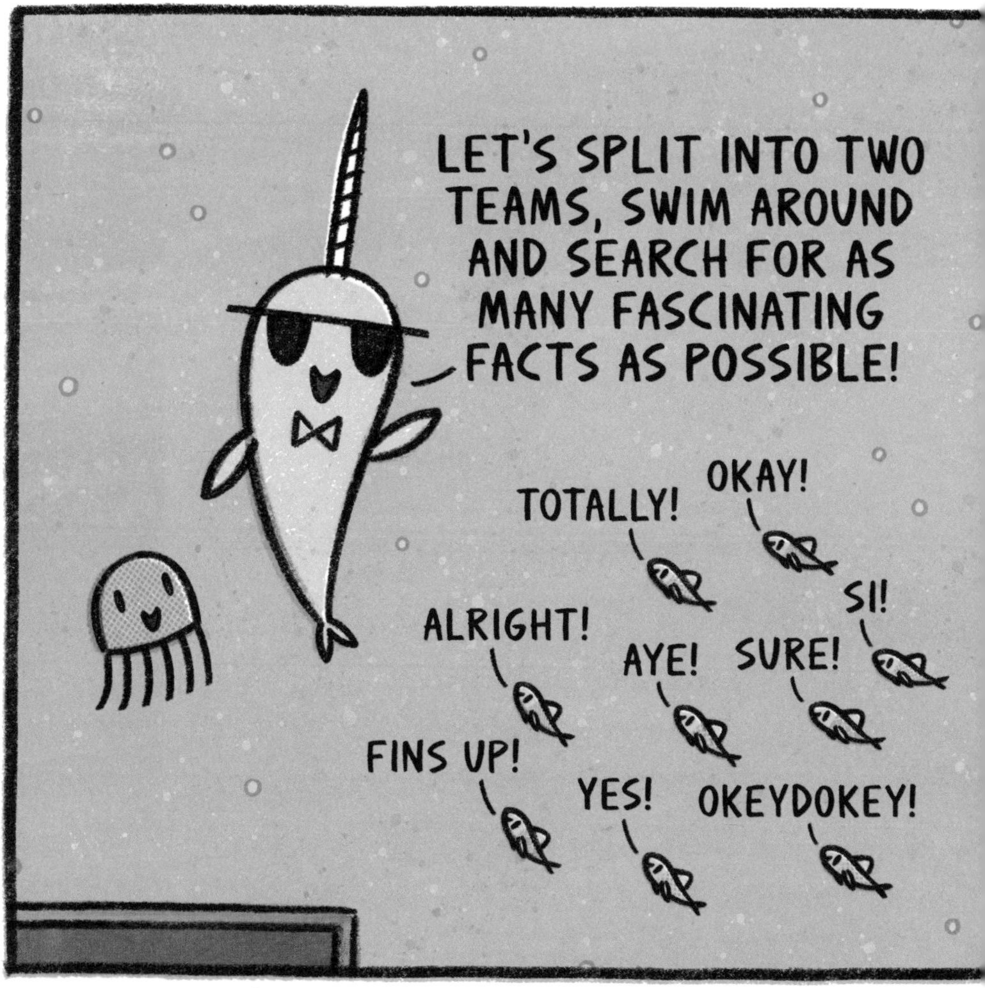
LET'S SPLIT INTO TWO TEAMS, SWIM AROUND AND SEARCH FOR AS MANY FASCINATING FACTS AS POSSIBLE!
TOTALLY!
OKAY!
SI!
ALRIGHT!
AYE!
SURE!
FINS UP!
YES!
OKEYDOKEY!

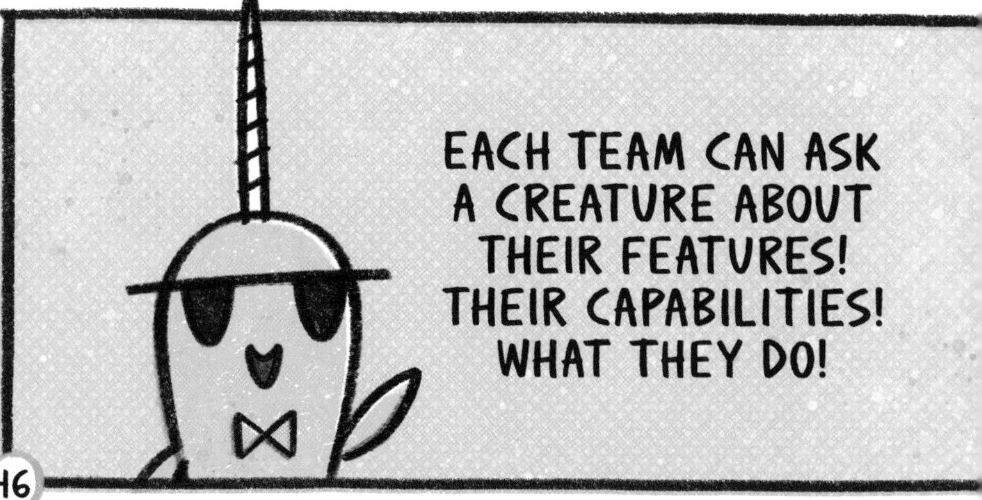
EACH TEAM CAN ASK A CREATURE ABOUT THEIR FEATURES! THEIR CAPABILITIES! WHAT THEY DO!

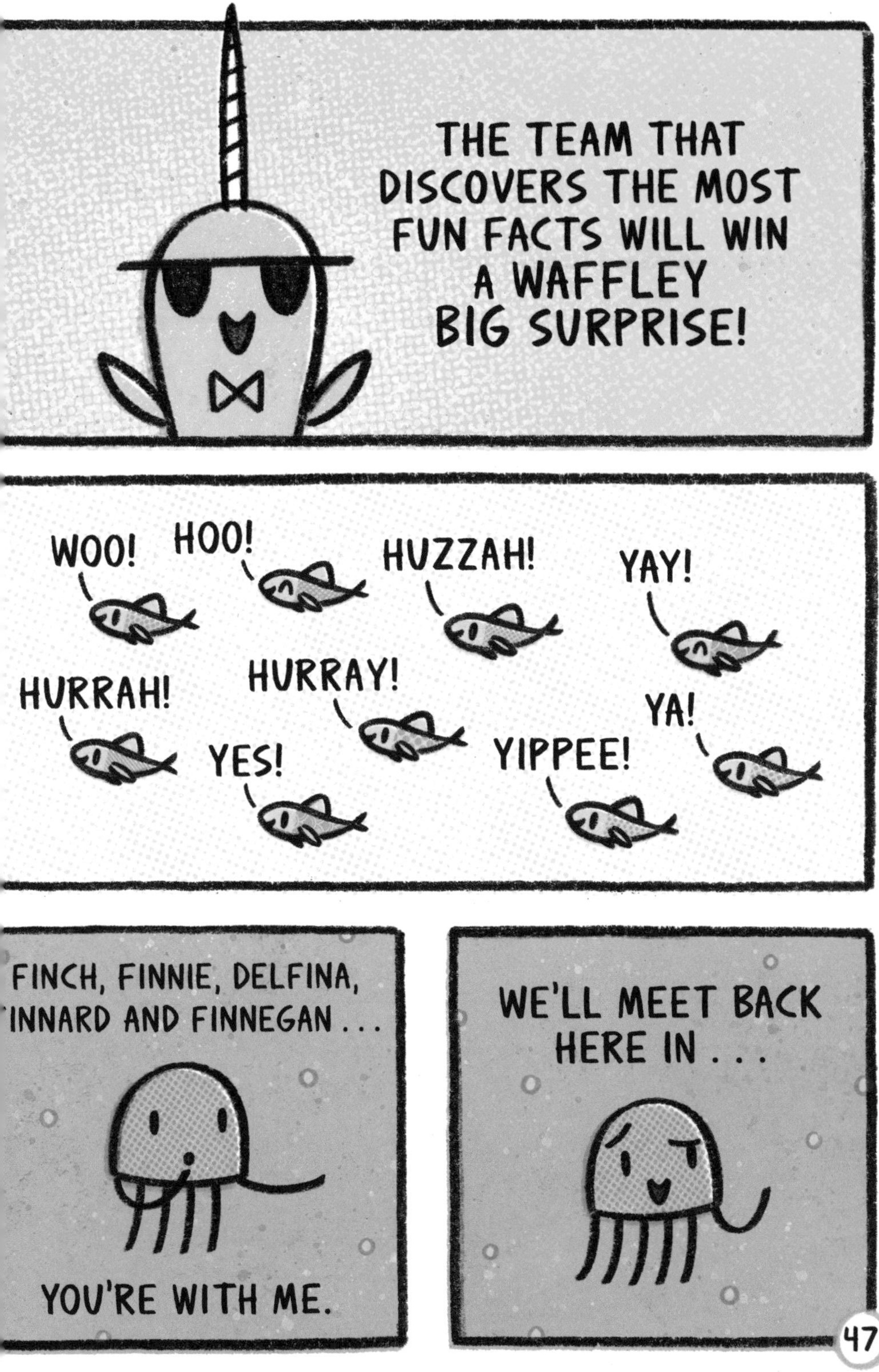
THE TEAM THAT DISCOVERS THE MOST FUN FACTS WILL WIN A WAFFLEY BIG SURPRISE!
WOO!
HOO!
HUZZAH!
YAY!
HURRAH!
HURRAY!
YES!
YIPPEE!
YA!
FINCH, FINNIE, DELFINA, INNARD AND FINNEGAN . . .
YOU'RE WITH ME.
WE'LL MEET BACK HERE IN . . .

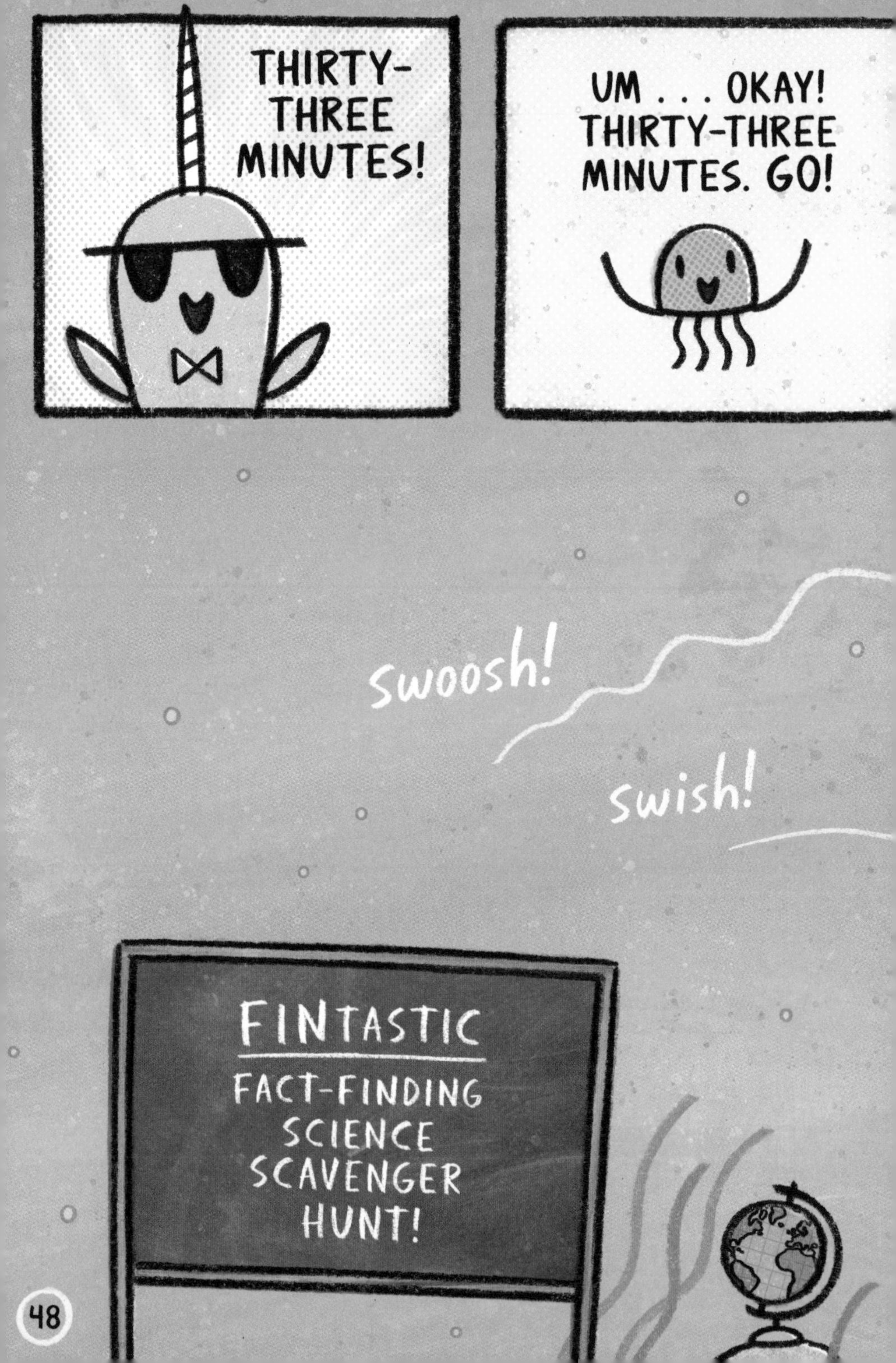
THIRTY-THREE MINUTES!
UM . . . OKAY! THIRTY-THREE MINUTES. GO!
swoosh!
swish!
FINTASTIC
FACT-FINDING SCIENCE SCAVENGER HUNT!

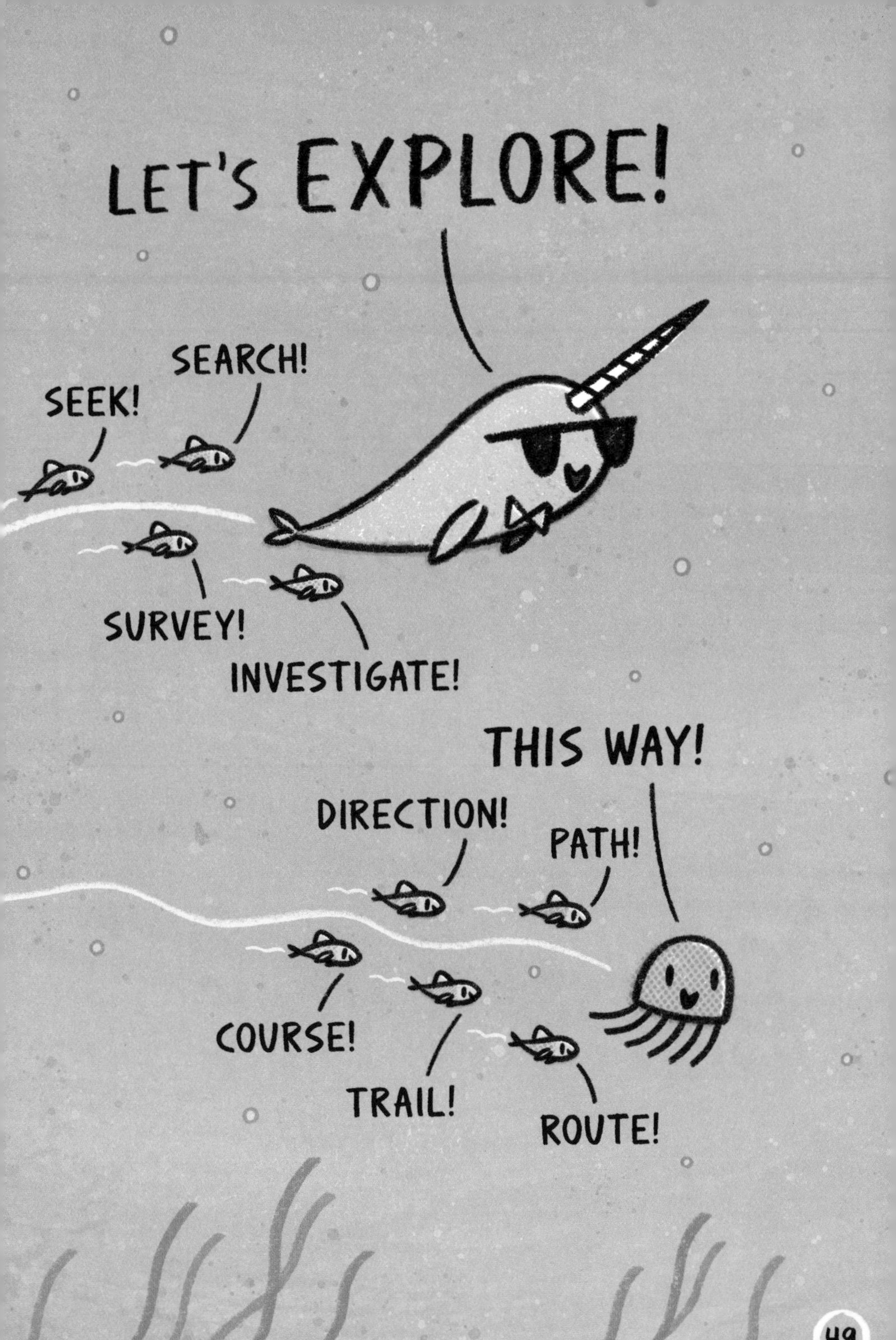
LET'S EXPLORE!
SEEK!
SEARCH!
SURVEY!
INVESTIGATE!
THIS WAY!
DIRECTION!
PATH!
COURSE!
TRAIL!
ROUTE!

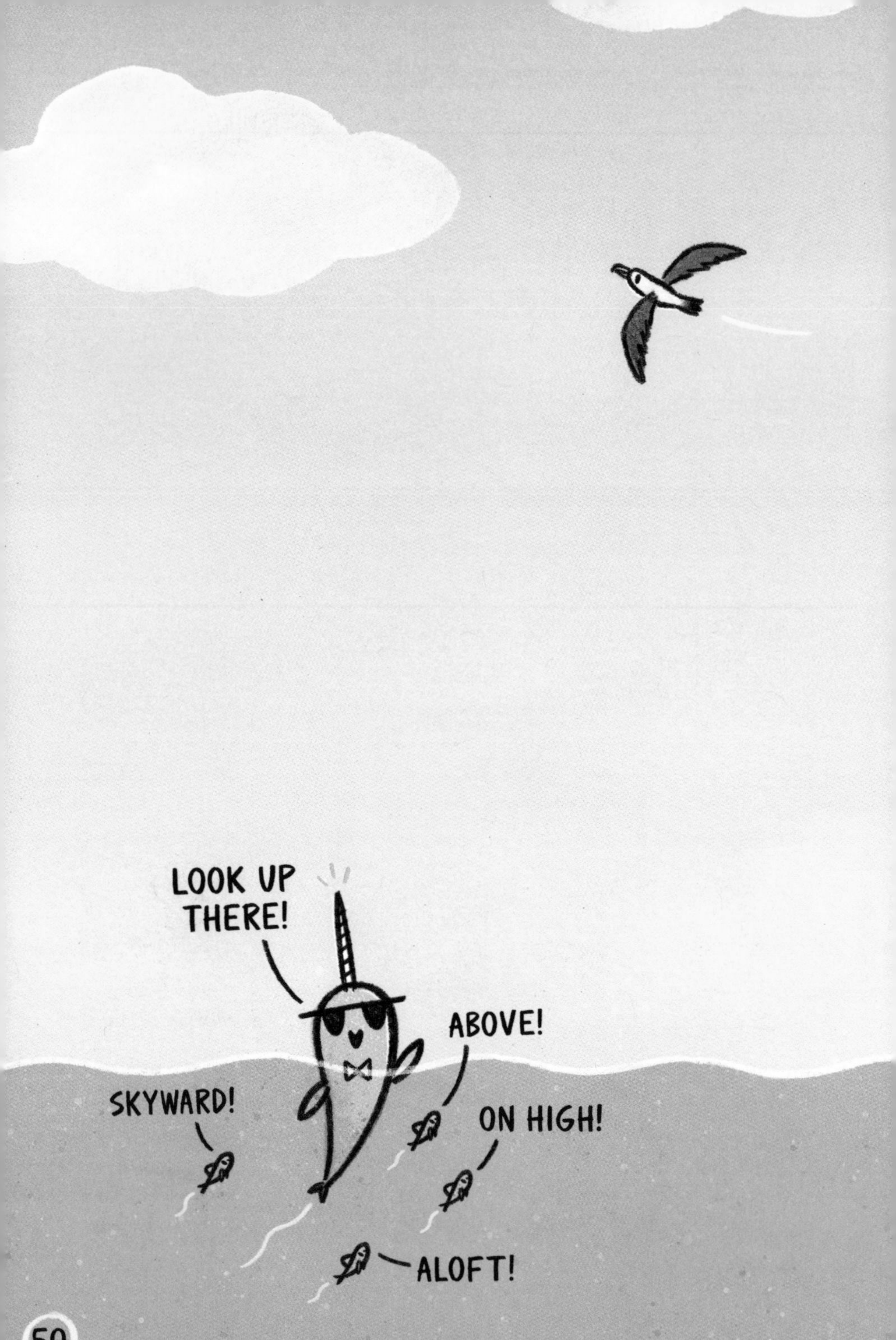
LOOK UP THERE!
ABOVE!
SKYWARD!
ON HIGH!
ALOFT!

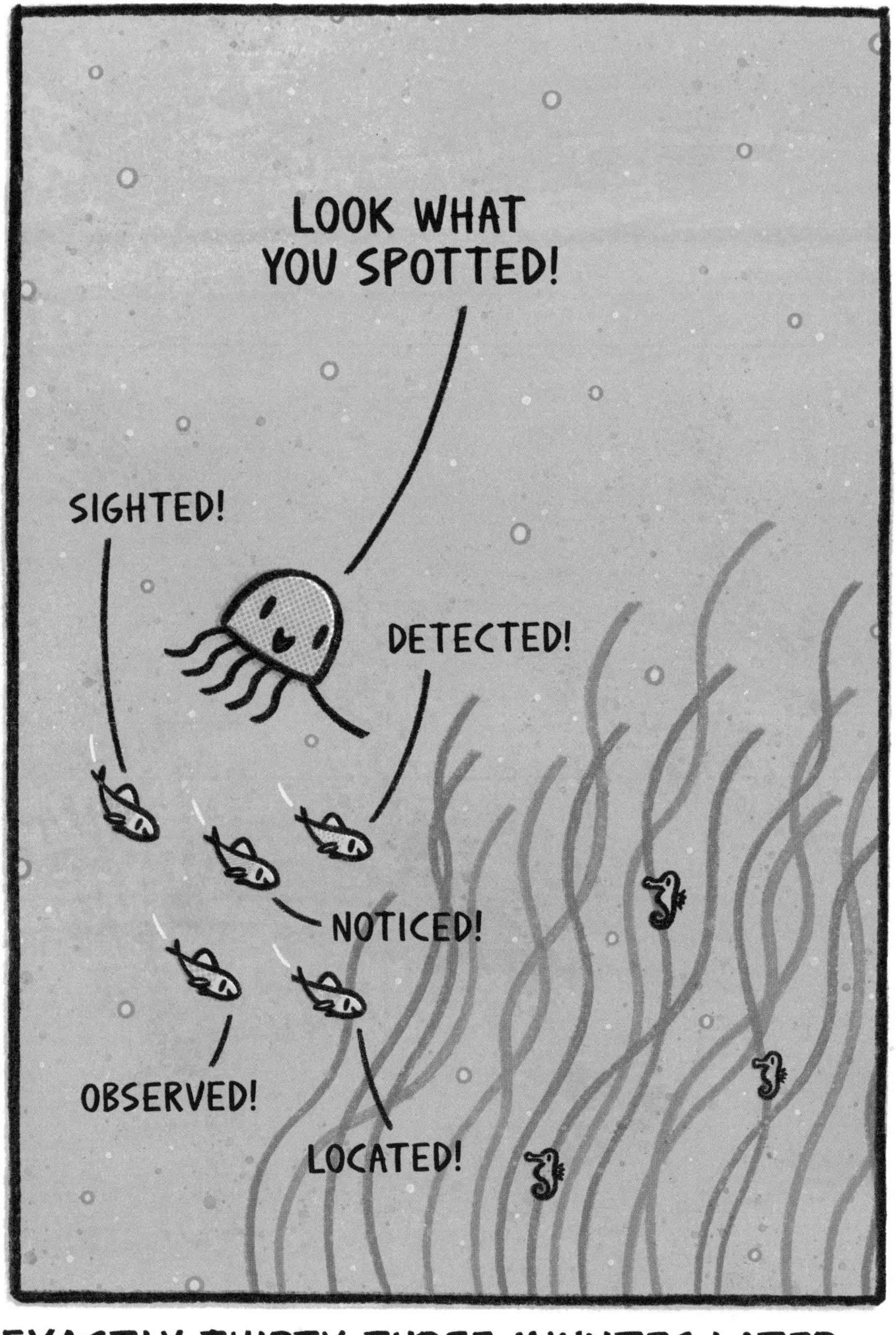
LOOK WHAT YOU SPOTTED!
SIGHTED!
DETECTED!
NOTICED!
OBSERVED!
LOCATED!

EXACTLY THIRTY-THREE MINUTES LATER . . .

THE RESULTS!

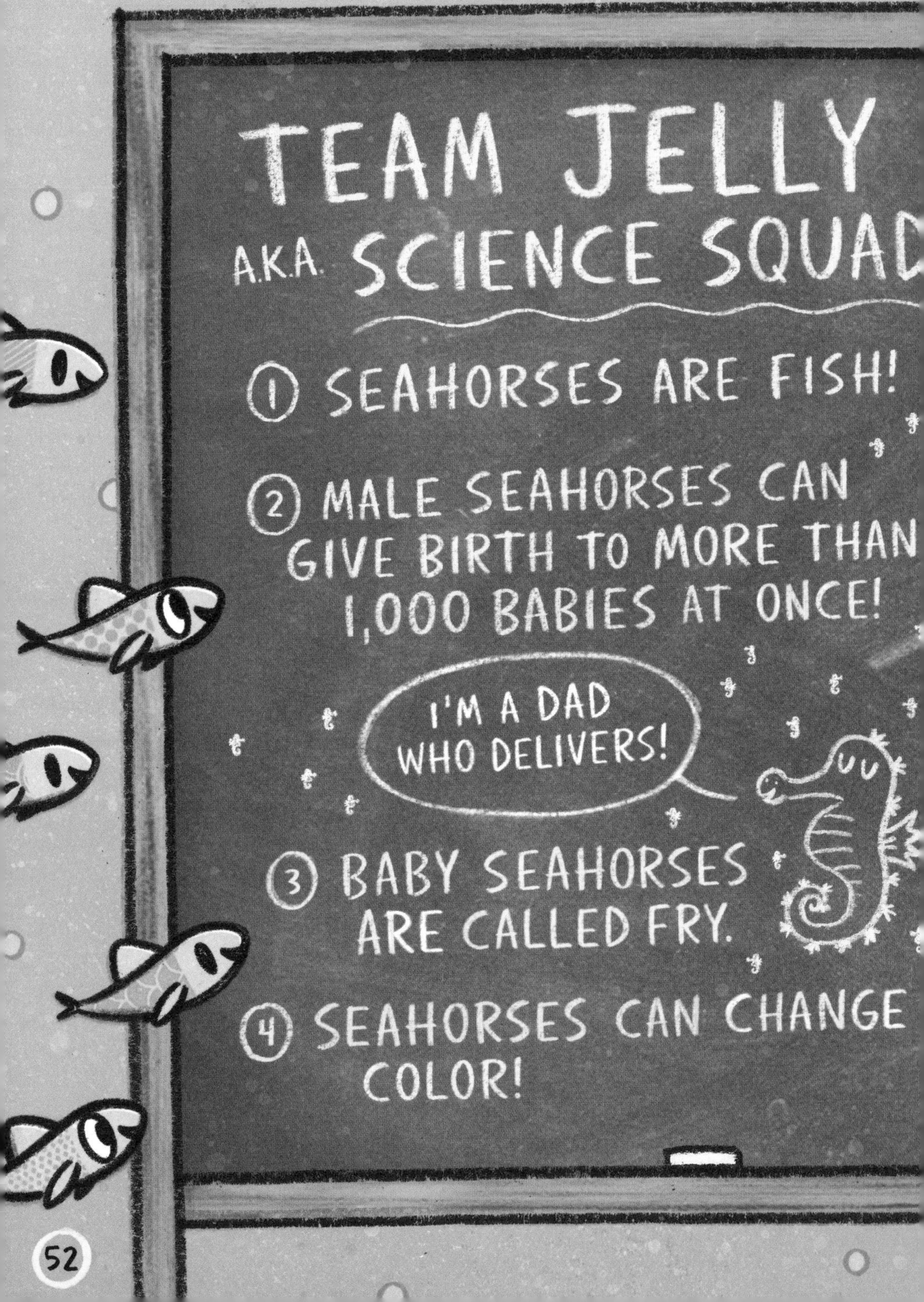
TEAM JELLY
A.K.A. SCIENCE SQUAD
① SEAHORSES ARE FISH!
② MALE SEAHORSES CAN GIVE BIRTH TO MORE THAN 1,000 BABIES AT ONCE!
I'M A DAD WHO DELIVERS!
③ BABY SEAHORSES ARE CALLED FRY.
④ SEAHORSES CAN CHANGE COLOR!